ENEMIES OF PEACE

From the author of
The Infinite-Infinite and Nailbiters,

M.K. WILLIAMS

Foreword by **DOUG NORDMAN**

"Why Brownlee Left" by Paul Muldoon. Originally printed 1980 by Wake Forest University Press & Faber and Faber

Printed in the United States of America

First Printing, 2017

Cover and Interior Design: Formatted Books
Publisher: MK Williams Publishing, LLC
Library of Congress Control Number: 2017915014

ISBN
978-1-952084-32-4 (eBook)
978-1-952084-33-1 (Paperback)
978-1-952084-34-8 (Hardcover)

Second Edition, 2024

1mkwilliamsauthor@gmail.com
1mkwilliams.com

Works by M.K. Williams

Fiction

The Project Collusion Series
Nailbiters
Architects

The Feminina Series
The Infinite-Infinite
The Alpha-Nina

Other Fiction
The Games You Cannot Win
Escaping Avila Chase
Interview with a #Vanlifer

Non-Fiction

Self-Publishing for the First-Time Author
Book Marketing for the First-Time Author
How to Write Your First Novel: A Guide for Aspiring Fiction Authors
Going Wide: Self-Publishing Your Books Outside The Amazon Ecosystem
Author Your Ambition: The Complete Self-Publishing Workbook for First-Time Authors

Dedicated to Thomas F. Bissonette

CONTENTS

FOREWORD

I met "Enemies of Peace" before I met M.K. Williams. It's my favorite novel about financial independence. It may be one of the first novels on the topic!

In January 2018, I attended my first weekend of CampFI. I've written about personal finance and FI for over two decades, and I love talking with small groups of people who share my interests. (If we haven't met yet, please look me up.) I'd already been to financial conferences and a couple of Camp Mustache meetups, and I was happy to help spread the knowledge with a new meetup.

In what's become a CampFI tradition, the check-in table held piles of donated books about financial independence. I'd already read the others, but the title of M.K.'s book caught my eye. A novel instead of yet another how-to money manual? Strangely interesting.

Much later that evening (well past my usual bedtime) I made my excuses to the other campers and headed for my room. I was still buzzing a little with first-day excitement, so I decided to relax by reading a few pages before going to sleep.

Two hours later I was buzzing with exhaustion and had to force myself to save the rest of her story for later. By Sunday I was sneaking away for a few minutes with her characters whenever CampFI took a break. I was pretty sure I knew where the plot was going, but I enjoyed the scenery during the entire ride.

No spoilers, but I never saw it coming. The karma backlash is epic.

I spoke at both weekends of that CampFI, and on the second weekend I was stoked to meet M.K. in person. Since then, I've caught up with all of her books (novels and non-fiction) and I tremendously enjoy nerding out with her about writing & publishing.

"Enemies" is the perfect introduction to financial independence for people who want a better life. Instead of yet another book pontificating about boring details of budgeting, saving, and investing, M.K. shares both sides of the stories. We've all dealt with consumerism and debt, but she shows how we can be tripped up by our emotions and by poor financial literacy. We appreciate that her main characters have the best of intentions, and they really want to change, but their self-inflicted slippery slope is far more vicious than an overdrawn checking account. Meanwhile their neighbors seem a little unusual and might even be hiding a surprising secret. Cue the ominous soundtrack and the screeching violins...

If you're tired of being lectured by the financial media, take a break to read this book. Better yet, if you know someone who desperately needs to turn around their financial life, share this entertaining novel with them. When they finish it and they're ready to learn more, you'll be ready to help them.

And if your loved ones are skeptical about your FI ambitions, M.K. can help them understand your surprising secrets.

Doug Nordman
"The Military Guide" and "Raising Your Money-Savvy Family"
Oahu, September 2023

Five enemies of peace inhabit with us - avarice, ambition, envy, anger, and pride; if these were to be banished, we should infallibly enjoy perpetual peace.
- Petrarch

Give me your dreams, your diamonds, your swine
Sell me your freedom, forfeit your time
For you desire what you think is inside
But within walls and sheetrock – your hopes will never hide
Until you see through the haze and the smoke
Keep buying into me, bleed red until you're broke
You may escape me, but you're only ever out on bond
Beware all who desire to reside at the House on Hurley Pond

PART 1

Avarice

"O.M.G! O.M.G!"

The blurred and scrambled video was quickly righted and focused very closely on the face of a teenage girl with jagged bangs, acne, and braces.

"O.M.G. That was so scary," she spoke into the camera. A gust of wind whipped against the speaker overpowering the sound with a thick and harsh block of noise.

"That house is just-" a voice off screen, panting for breath between each word.

"That was just," the girl holding the camera began to try to elaborate.

"Keep running! Come on!" the voice off screen was insistent on continuing to run away from whatever it was that the girls had just witnessed.

Then a loud explosion, off camera. Not a pop in the distance, but a belching, roaring blast. The girl with the camera turned to capture the last of the orange and black balloon of flame as it deflated back to the source of the explosion. Both girls screamed.

"O.M.G." and the running continued. The video became more jumbled until it finally cut out.

It was a scrambled image, but it was nevertheless posted online. And even though there wasn't any substantive reporting of the explosion, it had received a record number of views and was then picked up by the local news. From there it was picked up by the national news.

chapter 1

HOT COFFEE. THE centuries old commodity that seemed to never go out of fashion, the ubiquitous and only socially acceptable addiction left in the modern world; his day revolved around that hot coffee. Loitering by the back door off of the kitchen with the pristine view of the wooden deck that had been installed the previous summer and the murky pond that seemed to glimmer in the unrelenting Florida sun, he took a slow sip from his favorite mug. It was bright white with an imperial mustache stamped in black across the front. A gift from a friend with an online Etsy shop, he had reduced his once vast but unremarkable collection of mugs down to just this one. His wife kept the matching mug with bright pink lips.

Sunday mornings were sacred in their household, a quiet time to relax before the errands began and the preparations for the workweek would be made. But first, coffee. Savoring the next sip, he heard his wife coming down the stairs.

"It's live!" she intoned brightly as she crossed over to the kitchen counter to begin preparing breakfast.

"Thank you," he said, still staring out at the view. "Hope there wasn't too much to edit."

"Not at all." She pushed down two pieces of whole wheat bread into the toaster. "I think it is one of your best pieces yet."

Finally turning to greet her with a smile, "Really? Thanks!" She still adored his slightly self-conscious mannerisms, how he questioned whether what he wrote would be good enough. She recalled that when he finished his first marathon, he quickly began to scrutinize his splits, not letting the thrill of his achievement sink in for a week.

3

"Of course, I can feel us working up to the big announcement." She poured herself a mug of coffee and joined her husband at the glass door to look out on their beautiful property. "I think the keywords you were able to drop in were excellent too."

"You're the expert with that stuff. I didn't even know I was using any."

"Oh yeah. You had 'consumerism', 'western culture', 'revolution', 'action steps', 'ways to get involved', and 'how to change the world' multiple times. In addition, you used the standard ones like 'fire', 'hacking', and a few others that are picked up easily. Those all play well with the search engines."

"Hmm, cool," he raised his mug in a mock toast to his wife.

"Yeah, when we look at the traffic this evening, I'll show you some of the metrics on the dashboard. We're getting a lot more international traffic too, which is great." She rattled off these phrases as though they were part of a second, secret language.

No one who knew them really knew what they were up to; they did their best to keep their online profile anonymous, but anyone who really wanted to could have found them with a few simple clicks. They referenced their first names and city enough times that it could be riddled out. And their online handle was eponymous, some of their associates in their web community knew their full names, address, and their motivations for bringing their message to the world. The idea of going global was a dream, a mirage, leading others like them ever forward in a vast desert of online attention. Somehow, they had managed to rise above the rest of the blog chatter and spark an idea within many of their faithful followers. They had the attention of thousands who were happy to follow their example. If they could really drive up their global audience, there was no telling just how far their words would be carried.

"Bringing the message worldwide, huh?" He wrapped his arm around his wife, giving her a sweet embrace as they savored that moment.

"You betcha," she let her head fall easily onto his shoulder, her long, delicate hair cascading across his arm.

"But will they actually follow what we're asking them to do?" The weight of his philosophical question pulled on her thoughts, forcing her to pause.

"We can't control that. If they decide to take action, great. If they reach out to us for insight and advice, amazing. But if all we ever do is what we are planning, then that has to be enough." She reached out for his hand.

He accepted. He knew that she was right; they could only hope that those who were reading their words would actually follow through on the action steps that they were outlining.

They could only dream of starting a real revolution, but he still wanted it. He could be perfectly fine just knowing that they were about to put their plan into action, but he hoped, he very naively wished, that others would follow their example. For their own prosperity, and for a realistic chance to save society.

A loud popping sound went off, catching them both by surprise.

"Toast is ready!" she intoned, pretending that she hadn't just been startled by the toaster. The loud sound shouldn't have scared her at all. But she was on edge. With the big day coming up she was feeling tense, her to-do lists had multiplied and failed to contain all that she knew had to be done.

"Excellent!" he finished the last of his coffee and reached for the ripe avocado that was on the counter. He began to cut into it as his wife grabbed the plates.

"I think I saw a 'FOR SALE' sign go up next door," she threw out this information as though it were the expiration date on a carton of milk.

"Huh," he barely contained his ire. "Well, that didn't take long."

"Nope," she rolled her eyes and passed the salt and pepper over to her husband. He let out a sigh.

"We can't control this; we will move forward and hope that it won't impact our plan." She patted his arm as he stood, keeping his arm still until he regained his calm. He accepted her advice and continued until the avocado was in two halves. He mashed it onto the toast and ate a peaceful breakfast with his wife. He hoped that the closing would go quickly and that the new neighbors would move in and settle down in record time. This was indeed a significant wrinkle in their plan, the one that had been years in the making. He knew that they needed this to go smoothly. He needed that house filled and a lively, attractive, young couple to live there.

chapter 2

I T WAS A Sunday much like the rest for the young and ill-fated Lawsons. With venti Starbucks lattes in hand, they were prepared to look at a few houses, one of which they hoped would be their new home. This weekend was different, this day more important. Rather than viewing homes on HGTV, they would be squired about town. A realtor would take them to look into houses, walk on their floors, and scrutinize their superficial details. A year into their young marriage, Timothy and Cynthia Lawson were ready to move out of their cramped apartment and take on the next big step in life: owning a home.

Cynthia dressed in her nicest casual outfit to look the part of the moderately affluent wife. She modeled her style after all of the picky wives she had seen on countless hours of television programming around the house-buying process. *They say that you should dress for the job that you want, not the one that you have.* Well, Cynthia was mimicking that advice in her personal life; she wanted her and Timothy to be a well-off young couple that had the clear visual cues of success. Her deep, chocolatey brown hair was always perfectly coiffed; her expensive haircut usually necessitated a regimen of styling, drying, curling, and a cocktail of serums and sprays. Cynthia's naturally olive-toned skin, an inheritance from her Southern-European ancestors, was tanned and lotioned. While her forearms were smooth and soft, her neck was starting to show the first signs of age. Those thin little lines were forming on the skin in front of the hyoid bone, threatening to make themselves visible through the bronzer that she had delicately applied earlier that morning.

Of course, she was wearing heels, even though Timothy had strongly urged her to wear comfortable shoes.

"We'll be on our feet all day looking at different houses, most of them empty so they won't have any place for you to rest when they start to hurt," he admonished her as they left their apartment.

Cynthia waved his comment off and maintained her selected footwear. She was only five feet and two inches. In spite of her dogged confidence in her looks, she refused to be seen in public at her natural height. Even her sneakers had extra padding on the bottom of them so that she could look taller when she worked out.

Timothy shook his head as they waited for the realtor to meet them; he was just counting down the seconds until his wife first complained about a pain in her toes. Together, they had come to an unspoken agreement that they would buy a home after they were married. As the one-year anniversary date loomed closer, Timothy noticed Cynthia's comments and unsubtle hints that it was time to make the move. After the top tier of their wedding cake was consumed and their anniversary dinner photographed and sent out to all of their closest friends and vaguest acquaintances on social media, he could no longer postpone.

Timothy asked around for a recommendation on a trusted realtor and that is why, on that particular Sunday morning, they were up bright and early with a full dossier of homes to visit.

He let his mind wander as they waited, not wanting to stir up any excitement or discontent about the process before it began. He was nervous that Cynthia would love every house, locking them in a state of indecision. He was equally worried that she might hate every house, and as he thought about that prospect, he realized that he could have the same reaction. Timothy didn't want to let Cynthia see him get worried over that thought. He focused on not letting his white-blonde and nearly invisible eyebrows furrow and keeping the muscles in his forehead from contracting. His ivory white skin was still blanched and burned from their previous weekend on the water with his uncle who happened to own a boat. Timothy's arms were gently folded for this reason as the burn was just starting to ease.

It would be the last sunburn he would ever experience, but he didn't know that.

His head of curly white-blond hair was covered by a red baseball cap to prevent any further scalp burn. Cynthia was not happy that Timothy was dressed like a man about to go to a sporting event for this auspicious day.

He looked like a man who could only afford to rent, she thought that they should both project that they would be able to afford a house within their stated price range. She eyed him and subtly, almost imperceptibly, shook her head. As Timothy inspected his hands for signs of the burn starting to peel, a large SUV pulled up nearby.

They were instructed to meet in the parking lot of the local grocery store. It was a location convenient to the Lawson's current residence. This spot also happened to be the go-to meeting place for their realtor who did not lease any office space for his real-estate business.

The Lawsons were in the market for a new home, new to them, but preferably never lived in. Cynthia Lawson was adamant on this point. She wanted to work with an established development company and design their first home together. And by designing their home, she would actually be selecting from a pre-arranged list of options, each variation already likely to be in existence. Cynthia elected to gloss over that note in her mind as she daydreamed of getting her dream home. But, Timothy had insisted that they start their search by looking at homes that were currently on the market.

Timothy Lawson was looking for a nice home, one that would make his wife happy and satisfy their tastes. And by *their* tastes, he knew it was really *hers*. And by her taste, it was really just the things she had seen over and over again on television. Open floor plans, stainless steel kitchen appliances, hardwood flooring, stone pavers on the front walkway laid out in an inviting design. Mr. Lawson wasn't opposed to living in a house that had already been owned, or perhaps that might require some work. He wanted an opportunity to try out his tool collection, which was gathering dust and sorely neglected in their off-site storage unit across town.

The apartment was small and unsophisticated according to Cynthia. For months, she had been pushing for the opportunity to seek bank pre-approval on a mortgage.

"I'm ready to start living like a *real* married couple, Tim! With a house and eventually children!" She had patronized him only a few times. After the many hard-won battles they had experienced while arranging their wedding, Mr. Timothy Lawson had learned to yield early to his wife's desires rather than risk a fiery argument. She was rather like a toddler when things did not go her way, she would pout and stomp her right foot decisively. In the beginning, Timothy found that cute, now it was a tired routine.

Of course, Cynthia didn't think that what she did was childish, she needed to convey her emotions and make her husband understand that her vision of forever included a 'starter' home of McMansion proportions. Shouldn't he want to give her all of the things she desired? Shouldn't he want to spoil her and make her the happiest woman on Earth?

Nevertheless, with their seasonal lattes in hand, they had waited patiently in the nearly empty parking lot to meet with their realtor: Handel Smoot. Handel was a bit older and had a pronounced donut of a gut that would always pull at the fabric of his button-down shirts. He had previously been in construction and then worked as a handyman before getting his real estate license. Because of this, he offered a different perspective from what modifications could and couldn't be made to a house, what the rough cost could be, and, naturally, offered his services when requested. Handel's thick head of gray hair bobbed in rhythm with his steps as he got out of his large SUV and walked over to the Lawsons. He had the kind of gray hair that had a distinct, but inviting, smell of cigarette ash when it was wet, but would dry smooth and clear.

"Howdy," Handel waved and gave his most folksy greeting.

"Hi," and "Hello," the Lawsons responded at the same time.

"Well, are you ready to find your home?" Handel clapped his hands together and rubbed them. Cynthia was sizing him up, would this be a man that could find a great deal on a fabulous house? Or, would he talk Timothy into a "fixer-upper" that could never fully be fixed? Handel's chambray button-down paired with blue jeans that had only one shade of difference between them did not give her much confidence in his ability to find the house of *her dreams*. She offered a sweet smile, but inwardly felt her anticipation deflate. *This day will be a waste*, her mind was made up already.

The three of them headed out in Handel's SUV. They started their morning at a ranch that was built in the early 1970s. Even with the updated interior by the previous owner, Cynthia refused to give the home a chance. Timothy liked the price and thought that the location was ideal for their commute to work. Handel pointed out the upgrades to that home over the others in the neighborhood. Cynthia remained silent and passed through each room quickly. She didn't let any of the potential settle into her imagination. While Timothy began to picture cookouts on the porch and a playroom for future children in the large room off the kitchen, Cynthia eyed the crown molding on the walls and shrugged.

They moved on to the second house on their tour, situated in a highbrow development that had sprung up where there had once been a vast farmland not three years earlier. The properties closest to the entrance were townhomes and that neighborhood was considered a bit dodgier than the rest of the planned community. The homes in the middle of the main drive were nice and very packed in. After fifteen minutes, they finally reached the upper echelon of the development with large homes set apart from each other. The homes sat on large mounds of earth, formed by the construction company and had eventually, with enough irrigation and fertilizer, sprouted lush grass. Cynthia was giddy with delight as her eyes passed over each property. She could picture glamorous lawn parties and perfect Christmas-portraits in the entryways of these homes.

She didn't pay attention to the conversation Handel was having with Timothy regarding the HOA and CDD fees and other acronyms that she wasn't very familiar with. She felt mildly insecure that she was earning a meager salary compared to Timothy's six-figure income. Cynthia knew that for all of the demands that she was making, it was ultimately Timothy's decision as to which home they would purchase. But they were married and it was now their joint income. She tried to convince herself to think of it that way.

As they pulled into the driveway of the second house on their tour, more aptly described as an estate, Cynthia's eyes gleamed like that of a child in front of a toy-store window. She loved the architectural features of the façade. An actual architect would be quick to point out the mismatched elements, but Cynthia only knew what she'd seen in *Better Homes & Gardens* magazine. Timothy followed Handel up the front walk as Cynthia loitered, taking in the picturesque scene before her.

Upon entering the home, the chemical smell of the industrial grade products used to clean the house hit each of them in the nostrils. That smell, though noxious, was synonymous with cleanliness. It hid the odors ingrained in the carpeting and the worn-in stink of the pets that belonged to the previous owner. Cynthia smiled at all of the dazzling features. Such as the shiny brass fixtures that she didn't actually like aesthetically, but they sure did make that house glitter.

Cynthia took Timothy's hand and smiled as Handel began the tour. He took his time to point out the features of the home and the associated community.

"It's okay that you don't have a pool in the backyard because the clubhouse at the front of the community has both a pool and a spa." Handel commented on the amenities and the newly installed tile in the bathrooms, the fresh paint on the walls, and the ample cabinet space. Cynthia was sold on the home when Timothy finally spoke up.

"So, how much will this one set us back?" Timothy asked with a kind, but doubtful smile.

"This home is half-a-million dollars," Handel said plainly. He phrased it that specific way for a reason. In Handel's many years as a realtor, he'd seen hundreds of hopeful young couples, just like the Lawsons, spring for a home they couldn't afford. When the price was in the thousands or hundreds-of-thousands, the integers could easily climb without much notice. However, once he said the heavy and weighted "million," couples tended to stop in their tracks. Both Cynthia and Timothy were reluctant to respond.

"Okay," Timothy nodded his head and tried to hide the frown that was burgeoning on the corners of his mouth.

"Alright," Cynthia mirrored the same pattern and pace of her husband's bouncing head.

"It's well beyond your price range," Handel admitted, "but this is the only house in this area that meets all of your wish-list." Hands held out and shoulders shrugged, he paused. "I know when you are looking to spend as much money as you have in your budget, the last thing that you want to do is settle. But perhaps a compromise might make sense. You may not need to buy a home that has some of these features when it will cost you 10 or 20 thousand dollars in the final price of the home. You can buy a home without these items and add them on yourself for a fraction of the cost."

Internally, the Lawsons deliberated. "I do have some other homes that I think you will really love. They don't meet every requirement, but if you give them a chance, you might find your first house in this mix." Handel tried to offer what he could to the two young adults in front of him, they could take it or leave it.

"Okay, let's see them," Cynthia forced an enthusiastic smile. Timothy was stunned by her friendly demeanor. Usually, he would have expected her to state that she didn't see why they needed to stick to a budget, but here she was listening to reason. He gave her hand a gentle squeeze as they left the imposing and wildly expensive home.

It was also at this moment that their fate was sealed. With each step the Lawsons took away from the home that they could never afford, they were drawing closer to their doom. The path they were now on would, in fact, bring them to the home that they would purchase, but it would also deliver them to their murder.

The next home that Handel was planning to show the Lawsons was within the same development, but closer to the center of the community. There was little to no backyard and no space between the homes, yet each house itself was still 2,500 square feet or more. The homes on that block looked like cubes, perfectly positioned and evenly spaced. Timothy wondered how anyone could tell them apart; each façade was nearly identical to the next except for the combination of the exterior paint and trim. This stop was a no-go, completely forgettable.

They all clamored back into Handel's SUV to take off for the next location. Handel reclined in his chair and flipped through the notifications on his smartphone and the Lawsons mimed drinking from their now empty coffee cups. They needed something to fill their time and their hands, the empty cups sufficed.

"Hmm, you folks up for a change of plans?" Handel proffered in his game show host voice.

"Sure," Timothy agreed with a shrug. Cynthia was happy to oblige a change in the itinerary.

"Great, there is a house that was just listed this morning. It might be perfect." Handel turned on the car and started to navigate the local suburban roads. He gave some details about the community. Built up in the 1960s and while it was a lovely community there was no HOA, or board, or anything like that. There were only 40 odd homes in the neighborhood so it was small and everyone was friendly to one another. The top-rated high school in the state was only a stone's throw away. While the Lawsons didn't have any children now, they would be happy to know their future children

13

could easily walk or bike to and from school. Indeed, the neighborhood sounded idyllic. Even Cynthia was willing to give it a chance.

As the oversized vehicle turned off the main road, the avenue seemed expansive enough to comfortably fit the large SUV. There were sprawling live oaks dotting the sidewalks in such a purposely-haphazard way. The limbs reached across the road, arching to provide the perfect amount of shade between the leaves and Spanish moss. As they pulled onto Hurley Drive, the pattern of the streetlights changed from county-provided steel to a rustic black cast-iron with flare. The mailboxes all matched too. This made Cynthia smile.

They pulled around the wide curve in the road and stopped in front of the second home on their right. Cynthia and Timothy stepped out of the vehicle and took in the view of the neighborhood. There were a few children playing in the cul-de-sac at the end of the street while two women, likely their mothers, chatted in the driveway. The white washed sidewalks reflected brightly in the mid-day sun and the grass here seemed to be more lush and vibrant than the houses they saw earlier.

Handel was fiddling with the lock at the doorway and let himself into the home, giving the Lawsons time to look at the exterior for a bit. Timothy noted the decent size of the front yard, he would have to spend quite a bit of time mowing the lawn, but it was a heck of a lot smaller than the second house they had seen. Cynthia noted that the flower beds all look shriveled, but she figured that she could easily put down a little fertilizer and add some water to bring it back to life. She didn't realize how at ease she was with these ideas until later on when Timothy remarked at her sudden interest in gardening.

Hand-in-hand the couple walked up to the front entrance and stepped through the doorway. A quick breeze of air conditioning splashed their faces, as did the garish and blinding mustard yellow of the walls.

"I know," Handel already had his hand up in protest. "It is way too much of this color, but we can paint over it."

"Yeah, with a lot of primer first," Timothy responded.

Cynthia felt repulsed by the color; she actually felt a retching in her throat. "These ceilings have to be what, 25 feet high?"

"We can coordinate for a painter to come in before the first box is even unpacked," Handel was ready to smooth over whatever was necessary to get the Lawsons to see past the paint color.

"Okay, well let's see the rest of the house," Timothy gave Handel a nod of approval and followed him into the formal dining room, to the left of the main entrance. Cynthia lingered in the hallway and began to peer into the main living space: an open floor plan where the kitchen and family room seamlessly flowed. She left the men to their discussion on air conditioning setup and dry-wall and sauntered into the kitchen. Her manicured nails ran across the granite countertops with flecks of obsidian blended into the stone. She opened the refrigerator, which seemed to be relatively new, and ogled at the double ovens built into the wall.

A small hint of a smile crept up into the dimple on her left cheek. The obnoxious yellow paint was not present in the kitchen, where a red and white checked tile served as a backsplash above the countertops. The mustard did continue into the living room and appeared to wrap up the stairs into the second floor of the house. *Another couple gallons of primer*, Cynthia noted to herself as she crossed the tile floor into the family living space. This room featured a fireplace, completely senseless in South Florida, but a nice touch nonetheless. The wall mounting for a large television was drilled into the wall. There were a set of double doors with ruffled French curtains attached that let in the soft glow of the afternoon sun. Cynthia assumed that these would lead out into the patio.

As her hand reached to open the door, she heard Handel and Timothy coming down the main hallway. "You make a good point on the wind-mitigation assessment being an asset." Timothy was commenting on some selling-point that Handel had mentioned.

"Yes, it can take a good chunk off of your insurance which will save you a lot over the years." Handel was always talking about where to save money. Cynthia appreciated this, but was wondering if he viewed her and Timothy as cheapskates; that were just looking to save a little bit and cut corners.

"What do you think so far?" Timothy directed a question at his wife.

Cynthia spun gracefully around and flashed a big smile. "I actually really like it."

Timothy and Handel's eyebrows shot up simultaneously. "Really?" the incredulity in Timothy's voice could not be contained.

"I mean, obviously this paint has to go, but other than that, I *really* like it." Cynthia joined her husband at the island in the kitchen as Handel began to review the specifics of the home with the couple. Total square footage, price per square foot, all items that Cynthia was not concerned with, but details Timothy was intent on documenting.

"So far, everything you've told us about the house is amazing Handel. It was listed this morning?" Timothy confirmed.

"Yes, I wouldn't expect it to be on the market very long. Houses in this neighborhood get snatched up quickly." Handel was scrolling through his phone looking over some of the specs on the house that were available via his Realtor's network.

"Oh!" Handel stopped and called attention to a detail. "One downside is, no parks nearby."

Timothy smirked and nodded along, agreeing that this was a flaw.

"Oh, that's perfect! How is that a downside?" Cynthia blurted out without a second thought.

"Oh. Well, usually I hear from young couples that they want a park nearby." Handel proffered a response with uncertainty.

"Ugh! No! Why? So, kids can get germs and trip over drug needles?" Cynthia continued her tirade. Timothy nodded along; he never knew how strongly his wife abhorred public parks. "That's why we want a house with a big backyard," she showed both men with her arms, stretching them wide and waving them.

"Ah yes, the backyard," Handel's eyes began to dart around the room.

"Wait, there is a backyard, right?" Cynthia's delight over the house was slipping away like sand in an hourglass. That was a requirement on her wish list. *How could this bumbling idiot take her to see a home with no backyard?* Cynthia shot a look at Timothy that seemed to insinuate that she knew all along that this was a waste of time.

"Yes, there is. I think I can answer your question Cynthia by confirming the address of the house." He sounded almost intentionally guilty, as though he was being forced into confessing. It was like an overemphasized stage whisper. "501 Hurley Pond."

Timothy retorted immediately. "You mean Hurley Lane?"

"No, I mean Hurley Pond." Handel crossed over to the double-doors that Cynthia had just been standing at. He pushed both doors open at the same time and quickly stood to the side.

Timothy and Cynthia became immediately entranced. The stone pavers that built up a moderate patio gave way to a sprawling and open lawn that dipped down into the reflecting waters of a pond. It appeared that on the other side of the pond was a thick line of trees, but for those houses that abutted the pond, the view was spectacular. Cynthia knew at that moment that this was the house she wanted. Not only was it so mesmerizing to look at, but she also knew that it would just be picture perfect for their barbecues and house parties. Cynthia wanted to have that pond, she wanted to relax in the evenings with a glass of wine and stare at the sunset that would glimmer on the surface of the water.

"Wow," Timothy finally uttered.

"Wow, indeed. You see why it won't be on the market for very long?" Handel didn't need to explain any further. What the Lawsons were seeing was evidence enough.

"Yeah," a breathy agreement escaped from Cynthia's mouth without her noticing.

Handel let out a soft chortle at the reaction both of the Lawsons had to the view. "Shall we see the upstairs?" Timothy and Cynthia begrudgingly walked away from the view of the pond and followed Handel to the second floor of the home. A set of spare rooms with a shared bathroom and Jack-and-Jill doors were noted as a great option for kids. A side room that could be used as an office or even a guest room was sufficient and perfectly square. The master suite looked out over the front of the home, which was a small disappointment as Cynthia found her eyes longing to look at the pond just one more time. The bedroom was large enough to fit a small sitting area by the bay window and the master bathroom was truly palatial. Cynthia didn't ooh-and-ahh over the whirlpool tub and his-and-hers vanities as Handel expected. She was still daydreaming of the view from downstairs.

The three regrouped back at the island in the kitchen. It was clear that the Lawsons had found their home. "We can send in an offer today to get the ball rolling." Handel was starting to get out his notepad and was taking down the date.

"We have our financing approved for up to $300,000 so what is the asking price?" Timothy grabbed Cynthia's hand. It was an odd gesture for the two of them who were never overly affectionate. But it made Timothy feel like they were putting in an offer together, that by holding hands they were jumping in at the same exact time.

"The asking price is $350,000," Handel let out a brief sigh. "I think we can put in the offer at $300K and see if they counter. That should give you some time to clear a bit more with the bank or perhaps confirm how much you can put as a down payment so that you can finance the rest."

Cynthia's head was swimming. That was an additional $50,000 dollars that she knew wasn't in their savings account. They both contributed maybe a hundred dollars every now and then to that account. Where would they be expected to come up with the remainder? While she was thinking of how to scrape all of those pennies together, she also worried that someone else would come in and snatch that house up. The house that she was falling in love with. It had to be hers, *theirs*. It had to be theirs.

Cynthia looked at Timothy and gave him her most pleading expression. And then, Timothy uttered the most dangerous phrase in the American lexicon: "We can make that work." He didn't know where the money would come from either, but he hoped that they could do enough to get their lower offer accepted.

Handel put through the offer that afternoon and the Lawsons waited. They paced in the small living room of their apartment. Timothy suggested that they go out to dinner. He figured it would help take their mind off of whether or not they would get the house. Cynthia initially said no because they would need every last cent in order to make up the difference between the final price and what they could finance. But then she came to her senses and realized that one dinner wouldn't set them back too much.

Timothy and Cynthia toasted to the next chapter of their lives together over their nice hot meal. Their next chapter, and the last chapter, as it would seem.

The house on Hurley Pond and the Lawsons would soon be permanently united. Property tax records, FICO score security questions, return address labels, and fond memories. The house on Hurley Pond and the Lawsons would soon be inseparable, legally and personally. They would belong to each other. But something was rupturing, and corroding deep within both of them. There was nothing that stood out at first glance to make the Lawsons or anyone suspect that within their idyllic neighborhood a double homicide would soon be committed. Who would perpetrate such an act? Would it be a nameless vandal, a thief with a jumpy trigger finger? Or would it be the quiet and unusual neighbors who seemed to have a plan brewing?

chapter **3**

W E SHOULD HAVE actually started at a different point, but perhaps the science might scare you away. Ages ago, eons, epochs into the past, when this ground emerged from the sea and settled, it began to shift. Each rushing rainstorm pushed a little more sediment away. Each downpour did damage. Thousands and thousands of years before the Lawsons stepped foot into their dream home, the soft sediment began to slide and sculpt itself. Into the oceans it plunged, before it came up again even higher as a tall plateau before diving back into the deep oceans. The land only resurfaced as the majority of the water on the planet found itself imprisoned in thick continents of ice. The ground upon which the house was built was old, it had earned its spot on the planet and the small bit of acne growing upon it, modern American housing, would come and go quickly.

Or a better place to start may have been the birth of America. The fiercely independent spirit that spurred the Revolution and would later deteriorate into an inflated sense of entitlement without any concern for enacting change desperately needed in the world. The Lawsons were a standard product of their generation. Let's not use the word Millennial, it has a pejorative connotation that has only been abused and exhausted by journalists looking to stuff keywords into their latest article. Why is the housing market down? Millennials. Why is the economy stuck? Millennials. Why are people so rude? Millennials. Why did fascism spread so quickly in post-World War 1 Europe? Millennials. You name it, they've been blamed for it. So perhaps that term will unfairly bias you against the Lawsons, not that they are completely without fault.

Let's just say that they were post 9/11-ers. They were living idyllic American childhoods when their middle school English classes were interrupted with terrible news. They saw cousins leave for Afghanistan only to see part of them come back, their limbs devoured by the machine of war and hatred. They grew up accustomed to just dropping people off at the airport, though they could vaguely remember a time when they were very young and met their grandparents at the gate. Though not everything about the people they became was impacted by the event, much of their environment was shaped by 9/11. The Lawsons were a product of their generation.

Was that why they were so focused on the here and now? Because they worried that at any moment some anonymous terrorist would steal their lives? No, or at least not on any conscious level.

All around them their peers were defining themselves in the most over-emphasized manner. Their college friends weren't just painters or film-makers; they were shock-artists. Their coworkers were hyper-multitasking. Their mothers became extreme-couponers. Extreme. EXTREME. It was all so extreme. Of course, you can't forget the actual extremists, always bubbling just beneath the surface of society.

The Lawsons were only extreme in the way that they followed *the plan* so strictly.

Married – check
Designer dog – check
Luxury vehicles – check, check
House – (almost check)

They did what they were supposed to do. Their spending was fueling the economy, right? If they ever felt out of sorts about the items they were buying, they would simply tell themselves that they were stimulating the economy. The American Economy- surely it was feeding more people and keeping the streets safe more so than any small bit of charity. The Lawsons felt secure that their money was best spent if funneled directly back into the machine of the American Economy.

And perhaps that naïve, no naïve isn't the right word. Blind. Yes, per-haps it was the fact that they were walking through life with their blinders on that led them to that house. It's a foolish way to walk about, unable to see where you are going. You just might fall into a big, dark, gaping hole.

chapter **4**

T HE BIG DAY had arrived. Cynthia and Timothy Lawson would no longer be renters, subject to the whims of their landlords. With a successful final walk-through and the reassurances that the inspector's report had been thorough, they were ready to sign on the dotted line. Neither had ever purchased a home before, and they were aware of all that they didn't know. Was the lot size big enough? Was it ok that the roof had been replaced 7 years ago, would it need to be done again soon? All things that they weren't sure of, but they were eager to dive in and figure it out together.

Handel had picked up the Lawsons at their apartment to drive them to the final walk-through and then signing. The pair had spent the previous week packing and had worked all night to load up their oversized U-Haul with all of their belongings. They wanted to return the truck as soon as possible to avoid any overage charges. This meant that they had to work through the night to get every box, suitcase, sofa, chair, and dresser into the truck, much to the chagrin of their neighbors. All of their belongings fit, just barely, after a few alterations to how the boxes were stacked.

Cynthia had taken a moment to set out a nicer outfit to wear to the signing. She had been stacking boxes in an old pair of running shorts and a wrinkled softball t-shirt. She changed into jeans and a sweater after combing out her hair and setting it to look just right. Timothy was ready to just get the keys and start unpacking, but he agreed with Cynthia that he should look respectable when signing on to their first mortgage. The seller had agreed to a final price of $310,000, which meant that the home-loan was still north of $250,000 after the down-payment and closing costs. Timothy had scrounged up what he had in savings and had received a small (large) bit of help from his dad to meet the $62,000 down-payment.

Cynthia was beyond excited to see the house come into view as they arrived for the final walk-through. The house looked exactly the same as when they had first seen it, the grass was a little long, but otherwise, it was perfect. As they passed through the house, they noticed some small items that had been left on counters and in the corner of certain rooms. "Uh, shouldn't the previous owners have cleaned this out?" Timothy gestured to some documents piled sloppily in the corner of the room that would soon become an at-home office.

"Yes, they should have. We can bring it to them at closing," Handel scooped up the documents and made a point to collect the other items as they continued their final review. Cynthia didn't follow the gentlemen as they reviewed the home, she was gazing out at that marvelous view of the pond. Hurley Pond, the body of water just behind *their* home. She felt a renewed surge of happiness. Her elated smile was still present as Timothy descended the stairs and crossed over to the double-doors where Cynthia was standing. He wrapped his arms around her waist and whispered in her ear, "Welcome home baby!" She squealed with delight. She wished that they could just start settling in right then, but they still had to make it official.

Handel brought in all of the forgotten items in a large paper bag that he happened to have in the back of his SUV. The title agent referred him to the seller's agent, a young man named Ryan Moore. He couldn't have been more than 24 years old and clearly subscribed to the most modern trends in men's hairstyling with the side of his head cut clean and a thick wave of dirty blonde hair stacked on top.

"Will the sellers be present?" Handel asked, gesturing to the large bag in his arms.

"Hello, nice to meet you," Mr. Moore moved quickly to shake the hands of the Lawsons and make their acquaintance.

Timothy returned the greeting as his hand crumpled under the even and heavy pressure of Mr. Moore's handshake. "We noticed on the walk through that there were still some pictures and some mail at the house. We were hoping to hand that off to the owners at closing."

"Oh no, they won't be here," Ryan Moore said as he moved to gather his Styrofoam cup of coffee. "Do you need anything else from me?" he directed his question to the title agent.

"No, we'll just have the Lawsons sign and we should be all done," she reached out to shake his hand and he slipped out before Handel could stop him. He might have normally followed him outside to hand off the remaining items, but he needed to guide the Lawsons through the paperwork that they were about to sign.

The title agent presented them with coffee and donuts. The assistant offered to take several photos as the couple signed the papers. With all of the pages that needed signatures and initials, there were more than a few opportunities to get just the right image. Everything was signed within ten minutes and the Lawsons were officially homeowners. They posed with a red and white "SOLD" sign for a final picture that Cynthia immediately posted on her social networks. She would be posting a lot more as they continued to move and unpack, but now it was officially official with the announcement made public to the world.

Returning to their apartment for the last time, the Lawsons added the paper bag of the previous owner's items onto their own piles in Timothy's car and changed back into their grubby clothes. Cynthia renewed her complaint that they hadn't hired movers to assist, but Timothy bit his tongue. He could only explain so many times that after committing so much money to the house he didn't feel right spending any extra dollars on hiring movers. They picked up a drive-through lunch as they headed to their new home. Timothy rationalized that the small extra spend of $10 on lunch was small enough to not matter, certainly much smaller than the hundreds it would have cost to hire a professional team of movers.

The hours flew by and they got to work unloading the truck. Cynthia had her hands full with moving boxes into the correct location and keeping her little Pomeranian named Bentley from barking up a storm. She was ready to relax for the first evening in her new home with Timothy. Surely, now that they had a house that they both loved, they could truly live 'happily ever after.' Cynthia worked her way through the boxes in the kitchen, unwrapping the delicate china and the plates that she had selected for their wedding registry from their bubble-wrap. She placed them into the cabinets so that she could easily reach them.

With each plate that she put into the cabinet, she felt more and more in control of their destiny. She took the time to look at the small details of the design work on the plates: the off-white color against the teal and silver swirling scrollwork along the edges. She had agonized over which design to select when she and Timothy had been engaged. She remembered the frustration she felt when he kept telling her not to include any plates or kitchen items on their registry. *Didn't they already have more than enough plates and dishes and pots and pans?* She remembered sighing and telling him that he just didn't understand and that these plates would be more special because they were given as a wedding gift. They could just get rid of those old ones. (But those old plates had made the move as well, they were tucked away in one of the boxes that still needed to be unpacked.)

She remembered her excitement when she saw that two, then four, then six of the requested twelve-piece set were purchased from their registry. And she naturally recalled her frustration when the remaining six had not been purchased. Thankfully, the rest were offered at a discount from the department store so she could purchase the rest with the gift cards they received from wedding guests.

After the dishes were put away, she focused next on the wine glasses, the taller ones with the wider bowl at the bottom for the red wine and the shorter ones with the perfectly round bottoms for the white. She had a full set of twelve for each type as well as six champagne flutes. She had hoped for a full set of twelve flutes, but Cynthia knew she would work on upgrading their collection once they were settled into the house.

While the previous owners of the house had been tasteless in their choice of paint, Cynthia was grateful for the latticed wine rack above the sink and the stainless-steel wine refrigerator tucked into the cabinetry of the kitchen island. She wanted to put everything in its place, and make it just right. Next up were the pots and pans.

Spinning around in a confused stutter, the box that was very clearly labeled "Pots & Pans" was missing from the countertops. Cynthia passed quickly into the vast three-car garage. All of the extra boxes were cluttered across the floor in between the beach umbrellas and Christmas decorations. Earlier the sun had been shining intensely off of the white-washed driveway and gave the dark garage a bit of extra light. Now that the sun was setting, it was much darker and gloomier, she couldn't see the garage floor very clearly. *I hope Timothy didn't leave some box-cutter on the floor for me to slice my toes on.*

Cynthia hopped between the small islands of boxes and finally found the shiny brass and Teflon covered instruments. She hefted the large box up into her arms and stepped back to the door. As she reached the small step-up, she heard a sound from behind her.

Turning quickly, her perfectly shaded eyes were wide with shock. A man was sauntering into the garage.

"Hello, uh, just wanted to say hi and introduce myself." The man had greasy hair with sweat dripping off of the curls. His pot-belly was visible beneath his oversized t-shirt featuring a fish artfully leaping from the water.

"Hello?" Cynthia grimaced with the mock, plastered-on smile that she used on occasions when she felt forced to interact with people she deemed to be less *cool* than herself.

"I'm your neighbor, Dan. I live across the way. Next to Mrs. Schor."

"Oh, I haven't met her yet." Cynthia shrugged. Realizing that she had forgotten her manners, she snapped into action. "I'm Cynthia Lawson, my husband Timothy is somewhere unpacking." She gestured into the house with her head, the box in her arms still monopolizing her hands.

"Well, my wife Lizzie and I were eager to meet you. We'll have to have you over one night for a cook-out."

"That would be great, we're really happy to be moving into this community." Cynthia was actually sincere about this point. She was happy to finally be in their dream home.

"I'll let you get back to what you were doing, but I wanted to say hi. We were great friends with the Mahaskals, so we're happy to see another nice young couple move in." Dan smiled and the pudge on his cheeks obscured his small black eyes.

"Oh, you knew the previous owners?" Cynthia seized the opportunity. She put down the box and dove into the topic that was pressing on her mind.

"Yes, Tyler and Lindsay Mahaskal. They were really nice people, we got along with them great. They were close with your other neighbors too, the Ryechiks. They live on the lot next door." Dan gestured to the house behind him with his thumb swung over his shoulder.

"Oh, we haven't met them yet either. Uh, but if you know the previous owners," she stumbled for the correct pronunciation, "the Mahaskals, maybe you could help us get their stuff to them. There was some mail, most of it looked like junk, but a few things looked important. And there were some family pictures and things like that. I didn't feel right throwing them away."

"Yeah, they did leave in quite a hurry. We didn't even know they were moving until one day the for-sale sign went up and contractors were showing up every morning." Dan's expression became slightly pained. It was clear that the betrayal of being left out of the Mahaskal's move had impacted him. Cynthia could imagine her own friends might have been slighted if she hadn't shared the plans about the move. She empathized with the rotund middle-aged man in front of her.

Underneath that feeling was a thin layer of frustration. They may be stuck with this stuff or have to throw it out after all. "Oh, well if you hear from them." She let the words trail off.

"Yeah, will do. G'night neighbor!" Dan waved and sauntered back down the driveway and crossed to his house only casting a casual glance at the calm and quiet suburban street.

Cynthia peered out of the garage at the quiet street and spotted a woman in the house next to hers kneeling down to turn off the spigot. The next-door neighbors had an impeccable lawn. Cynthia was instantly jealous of their beautiful curb appeal while simultaneously sure that Timothy would be able to keep their lawn up to an even better standard. She made a mental note to remind him to call one of the lawn services that she had researched. She knew Timothy wouldn't actually do the work, but he would pay the right people and that was just as important in her mind.

Standing at the innermost edge of the garage, she pressed the button on the wall and the door began to slide shut. She waited until the garage door sealed closed before moving back into the house to continue unpacking. Cynthia felt a strange feeling of wanting to connect with her neighbors immediately, but she wasn't dressed for it. She wasn't prepared to make the best first impression. She needed to regroup and plan out those first encounters. It mattered. It had to matter, right?

Timothy set up the backyard right away, priorities. The lounge chairs were placed so that he and Cynthia could watch the sunset while relaxing. The small end table between the two chairs could hold their wine or books as they held hands and meditated on the day. They had never done this before, but surely with the beautiful pond for them to gaze out on this would become a regular occurrence. Timothy also set the barbecue up and connected the propane lines to the grill. He placed his locked metal box of grill accessories at the base, confident that his new neighborhood was so safe and calm; surely, he could leave these out without any worry of theft.

"Hey, there neighbor!" Timothy heard a voice call from behind him. He turned to see a man in a plaid button-down t-shirt and loose cargo shorts approaching. The man had a bottle of beer in his hand and an easy smile that was instantly disarming.

Timothy waved, expecting that the man was just going to say hello from afar, but he continued to walk closer and closer. "Hi!" Timothy said, as he walked around the barbecue and moved closer to the man, meeting him, not in the middle, but a quarter of the way.

"Nice to meet you," the man stuck out his hand, "My name is Jack." His arms and wrist had visible, but not bulging, veins traversing his subcutaneous muscles. The power in his grip was reserved and a clear sign of his physical abilities. Jack appeared to be the kind of man who could punch out thirty perfectly executed push-ups without a noticeable break in his breathing. He had the kind of hands that women would wonder about as they sized up his abilities: they looked capable, powerful, but not rough.

"Nice to meet you Jack, my name is Timothy," they shook hands firmly. Timothy was sure that Jack had the better grip, in fact his forearms were ridiculously sculpted, but Timothy didn't linger on that thought for too long. "My wife, Cynthia, is inside unpacking some boxes."

"Great, welcome to the neighborhood." Jack was gregarious. He was welcoming, and his warmth seemed genuine and not influenced by the beer in his hand, although it surely didn't hurt his amiable greeting. Jack had a bold voice, the kind that he likely had issues with as a teenager, as his child's voice squeaked and pinched on the way out. His visible stubble was another cue to Timothy that Jack was in possession of a readily available pool of testosterone.

"Yeah, we're excited to move in. We couldn't resist once we saw the view," Timothy gestured towards the pond which was just starting to shine red-orange in the early stages of the sun-setting.

"Ah, it is great," Jack said with a relaxed sigh, the sigh of a man who was at peace with the Earth and Mother Nature.

Timothy awkwardly wondered if he too should turn to face the pond and watch the colors change, or if he should reply with a question about Jack, or perhaps he should just beg-off because he was just not feeling overly social at the moment.

Suddenly a soft voice called from the distance. "Jack, can I get a hand with this?" The warm voice of, what Timothy assumed was Jack's wife, carried on the gentle southern breeze and alerted both men.

"Ah, duty calls. I'll see you around man," Jack extended his hand for another handshake which turned into sort of a low-five, hand-slap type gesture and then he sauntered away, beer bottle in hand. Jack climbed the low steps of the wooden deck belonging to the house directly next to the Lawson's.

chapter 5

A S THE LAWSONS unpacked and cooed at each other in their big home filled with boxes, the Ryechiks, their neighbors, commenced with their nightly routine of dinner. Jack Ryechik, the man who had so eagerly introduced himself to his new neighbor, was a man of distinct and well-curated tastes. He set the table that would host his wife's home-cooked meal. He poured himself a locally-brewed lager into a glass that had been stored in the freezer, and for Melinda, his wife, a glass of Moscato.

The house was immaculately clean, a point of pride for Melinda who neurotically wiped, and swept, and vacuumed. She could catch any loose dust along the banister and any stains on the baseboards; she disappeared the stray crumbs on the dark granite countertops and erased all spills before any evidence could accumulate.

Jack didn't necessarily contribute to the dirt and dust, but he was known to track a few unwanted items in on the bottom of his work boots. Melinda had specifically requested that he leave them in the garage before re-entering the home. As a dutiful husband, Jack obliged. He spent many hours in that garage, tinkering and perfecting his latest project. He liked to think of it as a project, it seemed more normal to call it that than what it really was. Yes, Jack had spent most of the weekend in the garage working on a project. That was something he could say when prattling coworkers pried on Monday morning.

At the end of a productive weekend, they were ready to relax and enjoy each other's company. The two lingered over their meal, taking deliberate bites and pausing to chat before resuming their ritual. They savored the flavor of the food and each moment. The days were flying by, but each minute seemed to be suspended in air. It was a golden time for the Ryechiks, they were on the edge of a major life event, they were at the horizon of the next phase of their life.

Perhaps your mind went instantly to the possibility that they would soon welcome a child, but that was not the case. They were not about to launch a new business, or graduate from a Master's program, or buy a car. The Ryechiks were dedicated to their cause and dedicated to each other. They had very few friends with a similar mindset. Most people, well, they just didn't understand. They usually didn't discuss their big plan out loud, for fear that just uttering it would leave them at the mercy of Murphy's Law. The weight of the idea might cause the air holding up the sound waves of their voices to collapse.

Jack and Melinda delicately danced around the subject as they marveled at the fact that soon their worldly worries would be nonexistent. They wouldn't need to fret over the small details that seemed to weigh so many down. They were invested in their cause and would live off of the vapors of their viscous principles.

But if you must inquire about the perfunctory details, Melinda was a designer and Jack was a financial data architect. They had been able to hone their highly specialized skills into lucrative careers that left them mostly fulfilled, but still longing for more meaning. They were college-educated, but had somehow managed to avoid the pitfalls that had ensnared so many of their generation.

"I met the new neighbors today," Jack added as he cut into the chicken on his plate.

"Oh, yeah! I saw the moving trucks. I didn't want to bother them right away," Melinda nodded along. Her vague and muffled southern draw would sometimes peek out around the corners of her mouth before she could catch it.

"I caught the man of the household as he was setting up the grill." Jack continued his story.

"Hmm, neighborhood barbecue?" Melinda hinted with a hope of one last blissful suburban summer.

"We can only hope." Jack finished before he plucked the sliver of poultry into his mouth.

"Well, if it does turn out to just be a show-grill, we can still whip up some 'dogs and burgers."

Jack smiled as he finished the bite in his mouth. "Ah, that is my wonderful wife!" The smile that broke onto his face was genuine and unexaggerated. He did truly believe that his wife was wonderful. Her voluminous thick hair was curling in the summer humidity in the most flattering way. The light of the setting sun was still straining to reach inside their open windows and cast a warm, orange glow across her face. Melinda was drinking in the moment herself; she could see the first few thin lines burgeoning around Jack's eyes and mouth. His handsome marks she thought of them. Jack was too kind to ever admit to catching any on her face when she would point them out.

While it may seem unrealistic that a couple ten years into their relationship could still be so blissfully in love, they were. Melinda added that sweet memory into her file and resumed their conversation.

"So, how was our new neighbor?" Melinda asked as she scooped up some remaining peppers and onions from her salad dish.

"Well, I only had a few moments, but he seems nice. Seems normal. Probably not a serial killer," Jack added with a wink.

Melinda couldn't help but start to laugh. It was horribly ironic and a perfectly timed pun. Jack enjoyed that he could make his wife laugh so heartily at his punctuated observation.

What an odd thing to laugh at, but they were odd people. The Ryechiks were nice enough. They waved at their neighbors when they saw them and made polite small talk, but it was always disjointed. When others would marvel at something, the Ryechiks would offer a delayed and halfhearted smile or congratulations. They had an idea. An idea, like a free radical, can spread like a cancer. They seemed out of step with what mainstream society wanted, and that made them a very dangerous couple.

chapter **6**

A NEW ROUTINE WAS born and with it all of the excitement and nerves that should accompany a new method. Our brains are hardwired to accumulate memories and habits, but they are separate. A memory is when Timothy recalls his fifth birthday where his mother arranged for pony rides in the backyard and a balloon-animal building clown. A habit is when Timothy awakens and moves through the same motions every morning without having to think much about it. Now, he needed to form new habits to match the new house.

Their new home was about thirty-five minutes outside of downtown, so his previous commute of a ten-minute drive through city streets would now be amplified and exacerbated. Timothy set his alarm so that he could have a full hour of drive time. He anticipated that it would decrease as he adjusted to the new traffic patterns, red-light frequencies, and general mechanics on the new route.

He rose that Monday morning and put on the suit that he had laid out specifically for that day. The rest of his clothes were still in suitcases that would need to be fully unpacked within the next few days.

He shaved and brushed his teeth in the new bathroom, admiring the spacious interior that could have fit their entire apartment within it. He smiled at the thought that his success had afforded him and his wife such luxuries. Cynthia was still asleep in the bedroom; Timothy was careful to be quiet. He kissed her softly before tiptoeing out of the bedroom and heading to the kitchen for a quick bowl of oatmeal. After cleaning up, which was exceedingly easy given that they had no dishes from the previous evening left on the counter or in the sink, Timothy got into his SUV and started to make his way to the main street and onto the broad boulevard and then to the highway on-ramp that would carry him into the heart of the city. Each step was something new that he had to focus on; within a week it would be second-nature.

The commute was easy to start, but became onerous at the exact junction that he had been warned of where the two local highways merged to funnel the locals into downtown. Naturally, or perhaps unnaturally, everyone was trying to get downtown on an early Monday morning. The broiling cars were all sitting, idling, pumping out gases as they lurched forward slowly until the bottleneck suddenly cleared without any new lanes opening. The oddities of the traffic patterns never made any sense to Timothy, but he usually didn't dwell on them for more than thirty seconds after getting out of a jam.

Finally, Timothy made it to the office at 8:30 AM, the same time that he had arrived at work the previous Friday and every day before that since he began working at the firm several years earlier.

The firm was Lawson and Lawson, Attorneys at Law. It began with Timothy's father, James, and uncle, Randolph, several decades earlier, and it was natural that Timothy would join as well. He hadn't questioned that he was expected to become a lawyer. He figured that it was a respectable enough profession, so he never objected to his predetermined career.

The firm started out by working on local environmental cases. With locally protected marshlands, reclamation efforts, and an estuary of animals whose habitats were also popular vacation spots, the firm had been busy. Timothy's father and uncle even experienced a small bit of celebrity in the early 1990s when one case was appealed and re-tried all the way up to the Supreme Court where they won out over a large conglomerate that had since filed for bankruptcy and folded.

Nowadays, the firm is primarily known for their kitschy television ads and billboards all over town. After the large win, the firm received inquiries from all over the state asking them to look into cases of corporate greed run amok, which then evolved into large claims of unpaid overtime and wage disparity, which further evolved into worker's compensation cases, which finally lead them down the road of personal injury. Technically speaking, they still worked on environmental cases, but the bread and butter of the firm had become ambulance chasing. By the time that Timothy passed the bar and started with the firm, he was left with the expired status of a once prosperous and respected firm. Now all that remained was the name, some small local celebrity status, and those God-awful commercials.

Surely, you've seen the commercials. Papa and Uncle Lawson in sharp three-piece suits, wearing eye-black grease on their faces to show that they were tough, or athletic, or had once played football perhaps. Then Timothy and his cousin, Henrietta, would come on the screen in similar get-ups and stand shoulder to shoulder with the elder Lawsons, all with their arms crossed and mean-mugs on their faces. Then James and Randolph would say in unison "You don't know the law- son!" and pause for dramatic effect.

Timothy was never quite sure what the message was that the commercial was supposed to convey. *That we're a tough firm that takes no nonsense? That we think we're better than you because we went to law school?* He never asked, and fortunately, the Christmas ads were always bright and cheery without any face-paint or intimidation tactics.

Timothy made his way from the large parking structure through the third story land-bridge into the high-rise where he stopped at the Convenient Café and purchased a coffee and the morning newspaper. After adding the exact amount of cream and sugar that he liked, he boarded the elevator with his fellow worker-bees and rode it to the thirteenth floor where the law offices of Lawson and Lawson were off to his left and the accounting offices of Dwyer and Hyde were on the right. Timothy often joked to himself that everyone would get a laugh that their floor had all the lawyers and accountants; it was surely an unlucky destination for anyone who needed to visit.

The new routine was completed and Timothy made his way into his office and booted up the computer. He sat with his back to the screen as he watched the sun over the bay and sipped slowly on his coffee, which wasn't that great, but wasn't that bad either. He had made it into work successfully and without incident, his neural pathways were already starting to learn the new routine that would be fully imprinted within the next couple of weeks. And after all, aren't we all seeking a calming force, a routine to keep our lives in order so that we can handle all of the unfathomable uncertainty and chaos of the universe?

At about the same time that Timothy was easing his way through the bottleneck on the highway, Cynthia was waking up. She felt a small depression in the mattress and realized that Bentley had just jumped up onto the bed. He rubbed his fuzzy fur in her face and she smiled and nuzzled him before getting up.

Cynthia had a very particular routine in the mornings. She would wake, shower, groom, pluck, cover-up, layer, contour, dress and finally after she hid every vestige of her natural skin and hair, she felt ready to start her day.

Cynthia had grown up, not in luxury, but in the appearance of luxury, namely in debt. Her parents wanted no expense spared for their little princess and they didn't mind the extra glitz and polish of the lifestyle that they had built. But the bills never got any smaller. They were careful to hide the debt collectors from their daughter, which was unfortunate because she grew up to assume that all money was easy money and that their lifestyle was easy to replicate.

When her parents finally came clean and told her that they couldn't afford to gift her a large portion of her wedding, she was at first stunned, then she felt hurt and betrayed, and then all of that internal angst broiled out of her like a dragon's fire. She blamed her parents for their financial misfortune, lecturing them on proper fiscal responsibility. The irony was completely lost on her, *her* wedding would now need to be financed from some imaginary fund that didn't exist.

She had taken out a personal loan (and then another) on the sly without Timothy knowing so that the initial amount that she had volunteered her parents to pay was accounted for when the couple began to write checks to the vendors. They needed that extra $20,000 to make their dream wedding, her dream wedding, come true. Cynthia had a secret second life where she would check that the most recent installment on that loan was withdrawn correctly from her personal account. The stress of the lie did bother her at times, knowing that she was intentionally deceiving her husband. *But it was so worth it*, Cynthia thought as she remembered that wonderfully beautiful day. As she passed through the new hallways, she thought of where she would like to hang the framed photos from the ceremony and reception.

She zipped out of the driveway and headed to the local Starbucks drive-through to order the usual to start her morning, a blended and whipped confection. Cynthia was addicted to Starbucks, or at least that is what she would say jokingly when she was exhausted or grumpy. "Gosh, I need some Starbucks right now, I'm so addicted."

When she finally did arrive at work, at the downtown building that shared a parking facility with the building that Timothy worked in, she sauntered into her desk on the fourth floor smiling wide, ready to answer questions about the move. Oh, and share pictures, she was sure that her coworkers would ask to see photos.

These patterns were actually the logical result of the life that both Cynthia and Timothy had been born into. It was the result of their parents' actions and habits, the advertising they were consciously and unconsciously exposed to, and the preferences of their friends that were reinforcing their own needs and desires. Both Timothy and Cynthia grew up in solidly upper middle-class homes. They weren't affluent or rich. They had each worked summer jobs through high school to be able to afford gas money, but they did have access to a vehicle of their own at the age of 16. They were aware that they didn't have everything, and in spite of the abundance around them, it gave them each a chip on their shoulder. They were de-termined to achieve more than their parents, earn higher annual incomes than them, give their own children things that they had been deprived of; such as private riding lessons and boarding schools.

And their closest friends all felt the same way. Begrudgingly grateful for what they did have, but continually striving for more. Because the American Dream told us that bigger houses meant that we had achieved success, we sought to take up as much space as possible instead of seeing the elegance of simplicity. Because that same dream implied that there was only so much to go around, we cheered for others to fail, but still expected them to celebrate the pyrite sparkle of our new riches. That very dream set up a firewall against any reminder that everyone on the outside of the American middle-class needed a little more human generosity. Because that would have meant that those who had achieved the pinnacle of American life were selfish and greedy and dare-say: cruel.

At the end of their respective work-days, the Lawsons went to their vehicles and drove home. They were within two minutes of each other for most of the drive home, but Cynthia took a detour to drop by her favorite little boutique, *Pro Invidia*. The store had sent her an automated text earlier about a flash sale for twenty-five percent off and she wanted to see if anything caught her eye. She was always keen to save, although the concept of saving one hundred percent and just not going into the store had never dawned on her.

The hunger for a deal isn't something that Cynthia should be judged by. After all, it is only human nature to want to save on a purchase. Perhaps what should be analyzed, is that day-in and day-out she drove past a man who lived on the streets. He usually set up in the park across from her office building at 4 PM to stake out his bench. While he looked haggard and aged, he was only in his early forties, a lost veteran with no home and unmitigated PTSD from the first Gulf War.

Timothy would pass him too, since their offices were both adjacent to this park, and he intentionally kept his eyes straight ahead. He knew not to look, not to risk eye contact. If he looked, then he would have to admit to himself that he saw that man, that human, making camp for the night in the rain or the broiling heat of summer. No, Timothy couldn't do that. Therefore, he ignored the man, and Cynthia did too. Both of them mutually ignoring him in their nice cars, burning twice the necessary gasoline for their daily commutes. Only once did they ever discuss the man, and even then, it was only to say that he should know where the local homeless shelter was by now. They made no efforts to hand him a bottle of water, or provide him directions to the shelter; they didn't even know where one was that they could point him to. They offered him no material goods, and certainly never an affirming nod or smile. They never gave him the dignity of acknowledging that he was a person. For that, you should judge them both. Not for their spending or vapid lifestyle choices, but for the manner in which they dismissed some humans and embraced others.

That doesn't mean that they deserved what happened to them, not at all. But it should color your commentary on this, much discussed and debated, tragic event.

chapter 7

C YNTHIA ARRIVED HOME to see the final purple hues of the sun setting behind their new home, the street lights emitting a soft yellow glow. She had, in fact, found a vintage necklace and matching earrings that she carried with her up the driveway. The cement was still smooth and even, showing no signs of the trauma to come.

On her way into the house, she noticed the empty cardboard boxes that had been cut up and laid nicely on the curb for trash pick-up. She rolled her eyes and huffed. Didn't Timothy know that was an invitation for thieves, a big bright neon sign saying, "Hey we moved in with all of our stuff, in case you didn't know it, but we have lots of stuff, please come take it from us."

She also knew that cardboard would attract other *unwanted* attention. She had learned her lesson about cardboard the hard way during a summer internship program in New York City. She had kept her empty boxes lined up near the refrigerator in her small apartment since she knew she would be moving out in just a few months when the internship was over. She didn't want to throw away the boxes only to have to scrounge for new ones later. One day she went to move the boxes and saw a family of *them*. Roaches. Bright, brown, shining roaches skittering away in all directions, spreading out. She didn't sleep a wink that night.

She kept the lights on non-stop for the rest of that summer as well, convinced that if the lights went out that the little buggers would descend upon her, feeding off of her fear. She would see them through the city and think *wretched roach*. Even when she tried to push the thoughts from her head, she would keep thinking it over and over. *Wretched roach. Wretched roach.* Soon it became a rhyme that calmed her and spooked her all at the same time. *Wretched roach. Wretched roach. Don't close your eyes, or else you'll choke.*

When her stress levels spiked, she would have nightmares about them. Throughout college, she and Timothy had lived apart so he had never really experienced her having this until he was in law school and they were first living together. Cynthia was stressed about telling her parents that she had moved in with Timothy, the nightmares of being attacked by cockroaches persisted until she finally spilled the beans to her mother. They faded away again until the planning for the wedding began. Timothy would wake up to her screams at least once a month. As the big day approached, they became more frequent. The days leading up to the final purchase of the house were equally stressful, causing yet another flare-up.

It didn't even make sense really. But this fear stuck with her. The cardboard on the side of the road brought the frightening memories back, her mind quickly spitting out *wretched roach* across her consciousness. She absolutely refused to live in a home that had even one; she walked past the cardboard, glad that it would soon be disposed of and made sure to remind Timothy to hire a service to spray regularly inside and outside. For termites, ants, wasps, you name it. But especially those evil little roaches.

chapter **8**

MELINDA RYECHIK HAD the pleasure of doing what she loved for a living. A natural night-owl and free spirit, she enjoyed the entrepreneurial benefits of her chosen trade. She studied graphic design and worked as an in-house designer for a local company's marketing department at the start of her career. She did this until she had gained enough interest from friends of friends to build up her own freelance business. And when the work got slow or she longed for a day-to-day with less responsibility for drumming up new business, she leveraged her contacts to get a full-time job with an agency.

Her work history was dotted with periods of regular work and then freelancing, which she would drift back into as she found the tedium of office life too straining on her creative senses. She was in the terminal phase of her current full-time employment with a mobile-first digital agency downtown. She liked the challenge of designing for teeny-tiny mobile screens and the projects were exciting, but she didn't like being told to show up at one time every day. She didn't like the strict dress code and the insistence on daily meetings that didn't seem to serve much of a purpose.

There was also the looming Grand Plan that she and Jack were working towards that would negate the need for her to ever work again. They didn't have day-jobs where she was headed. She found an uneasy peace with that knowledge. She had always been employed, even if she was just self-employed. The abrupt end to that pattern was unnerving, although the reason for it was exhilarating. Their plan was working, their goals were so close they could reach out and pick them from the vine, taste the sweet fruit of their efforts. But it was still a looming cliff, the date growing closer when they would make an irrevocable change. For all of the excitement, she was still scared.

Fortunately, Jack shared the same concerns. They had been talking about this idea for so long, and now it was all coming together. He assured her that they were in it together, they would navigate this new life that they were working towards as a team.

On a breezy afternoon, Melinda drifted downtown on her lunch break to enjoy a stroll through the city streets, her inner-urbanite in need of a good stretch of the legs. She walked to the park on the far end of the metropolitan district to eat her packed lunch. Melinda enjoyed the uninterrupted quiet, but noted how empty the park was during such a pleasant afternoon. *Why weren't more people out on such a lovely day?* She was certainly glad to not be overrun with overly-inquisitive children, or mid-day joggers, or her coworkers. But, it was still ridiculous that absolutely no one else was there.

On her walk back to the office, she contemplated a stop into the coffee shop that she would pass on the next block. She and Jack never purchased coffees, and they almost never ate lunch out except for very rare occasions. They had an austere outlook on dining-out that most people would balk at. But, in spite of their carefully detailed plan that required no deviation, Melinda found her mind wandering to the possibility of a tasty-treat with a caffeinated kick. In her mind, she resigned herself to just walking by without another look. Other women may dream of diamonds or designer labels. Melinda would be over the moon for an unlimited gift card to Starbucks, which she would use sparingly to make sure it still felt like a special treat. If it became a routine, it wouldn't be as fun anymore.

Melinda was just a few steps away when she remembered that she had a gift card for one free latte. The shop had been trying to drum up business and passed out the cards to employees in the nearby office buildings. There wasn't an expiration date and she had long forgotten about it until that very moment. Melinda stopped to sort through her bag, and there it was. The edges had curved from wear, but the offer for one free coffee was still valid. She grabbed her phone and sent a picture to Jack with the caption, "Why the heck not?!"

After she waited patiently in line, she heard her name called and her drink was prepared. She smiled at the other customers. Their moods ranged from indifferent to downright impatient. But Melinda was ecstatic, she was able to get her little treat without compromising the budget that she and Jack had agreed to. Her phone buzzed; Jack had responded. "Uh oh, late in the day for a coffee. What will you do with all that extra energy tonight? ;)" The winking emoji was enough to make her blush a little.

She savored the first sip as she exited the shop, knowing that she would be a little late to return to her desk. *Oh well.* She wasn't overly invested in getting perfect attendance at this point in her career.

As Melinda began to walk back to her office, she noticed a woman walking towards her, she was slightly familiar. It took her only a moment to recognize her, and she smirked at the connection.

Cynthia bobbled back to work after her lunch at the nearby deli. She balanced on her pencil thin three-inch heels as she tried to walk quickly to get back to her desk within the one-hour limit allotted for lunch. She popped a stick of gum into her mouth to wash out the taste of her tuna sandwich and crumpled the thin silver wrapped into a small ball and let it fall into the dark recesses of her oversized purse, never to see the light of day again.

She spotted a woman walking on the sidewalk towards her. This woman was tall, a tower compared to Cynthia even though one woman was in high-heels and the other was in soft leather flats. The sun radiated off of her hair and skin. The fit jeans and worn suede jacket complimented her. Cynthia felt instantly insecure in her too-tight pencil skirt that accentuated her little pooch. The woman was thin and beautiful, but more to the point the green in her eyes matched the shining leaves on the trees that dotted the sidewalk. Cynthia thought that this woman must have been photo-shopped, dropped inexplicably on the sidewalk. But she was real. And moving toward her.

Cynthia waved her head to move her hair off of her shoulders and reached for her cell phone. She looked at the display and punched through to her home screen, desperately trying to avoid eye contact with the mystery woman, the one with the superior looks that Cynthia immediately despised.

"Mrs. Lawson?" a voice of distinct grit and warmth asked, forcing Cynthia to look up. "I believe we're neighbors. I'm Melinda Ryechik. I've been meaning to pop over and say hello, but I've been working extra hours recently."

Cynthia feigned confusion as she decided if she should return the friendly greeting or simply regard this overly nice person as a total loon. She decided to be nice, since being friends with attractive people meant that she was considered attractive. She had read that in a magazine once. "Oh hello. Ryechik? Jack's wife?"

"Yes, I'll claim him," Melinda smiled warmly. Cynthia had already eyed her wardrobe and assessed her style and beauty. But things changed as soon as she spotted the latte in her hand. Or more precisely, she spotted her un-manicured fingers. Her nails were short and clean, but they were so plain and flat out naked. Cynthia tried not to cringe, but her face may have actually moved involuntarily as she noticed Melinda's smile wane. "I just wanted to say hi, I'm sure I'll see you around the neighborhood."

"Yes, I'm looking forward to getting the house all set up so that we can have guests over. You and Jack should stop by for dinner." Cynthia was trying to process the information in front of her. A beautiful woman that had great hair but didn't polish her nails. There was a perfectly rational explanation for this: perhaps her manicurist had to cancel her weekly appointment for some personal matter. Maybe she had spilled some kind of solvent when cleaning her house that ate away at her manicure and she was waiting for her regular appointment. Or she was a total nut job.

What was worse was that she recognized the slim plain gold band on Melinda's hand, that was her wedding ring. Again, maybe there was a logical explanation. Her diamond encrusted engagement ring must be at the cleaners. Maybe Jack was taking it in to have an additional ring of diamonds welded onto it. Good grief, hadn't Cynthia and Timothy just moved into a good neighborhood for the upwardly mobile? What would the community think if they knew such plain people had weaseled their way in to their neighborhood?

Cynthia's suspicions about the Ryechiks were born in that very encounter.

"Oh, we'd be happy to host. We love to cook dinner and it could give you and Timothy a chance to enjoy an evening without unpacking or organizing."

"That's so sweet. I'll check our calendar with Timothy and let you know," Cynthia was ready to beg off and get back to the office. She needed the input from her coworkers to sift through the details of her attractive but potentially weird neighbor.

"Great! And it seems like we work close to each other, what a coincidence," Melinda was being too nice now. She usually wasn't this outgoing, but as she and Jack had discussed these neighbors at length, she was excited to have an actual interaction on which to base her opinion of the Lawsons. Yes, the Lawsons were a very serious topic of discussion at their dinner table. The animosity that they felt about the circumstances of the sale of the house had stained their impression of their new neighbors like a deep marinara sauce. Melinda didn't want her hostile feelings about the Mahaskals to cloud her impression of the Lawsons.

Cynthia tried to shield her two-carat diamond ring from Melinda's eyes, she assumed that she would become envious and hatch a plan to steal her ring if she noticed how large it was. That her fear focused on such a trivial trinket is tragically ironic. If she only knew what Jack and Melinda were really up to she would have harbored no such worries.

"Sure," Cynthia looked at the timepiece on her wrist. It was purely ornamental as she hadn't read a clock face in years, relying on digital clocks to announce the time for her. "I'm running late to get back to the office, but we should catch up later."

"Oh, of course," Melinda reflexively reached for her own wrist, which was bare. She wore no watches or bracelets. She occasionally wore a necklace that Jack had gifted her for their fifth wedding anniversary.

"Bye!" Melinda carried on in her carefree manner, aware that she was definitely late at this point and she might as well enjoy the last few moments before she reached the office. Cynthia hobbled off, walking as fast as her tiny feet on stilts could carry her. She worried that she would be late, which would be a mark against her for a potential raise. She worried that she might break her shoes if she didn't watch her step. She worried that her hair was starting to curl in the early afternoon humidity. She worried that her new neighbor might be a weirdo that was oddly obsessed with hanging out with her. Oddly enough, she wasn't worried about the one thing that was destined to be her downfall. It wasn't something she had even considered or thought could happen to her.

By the time Cynthia reached her office building, she could see the elevator doors closing, just out of reach. She impatiently pressed the "up" button and tapped her toes as she waited for the elevator car to return. It was exactly eight weeks, two days, and twenty hours until Cynthia would die. She had 84,720 minutes left to live, how unfortunate that she spent any of those moments impatient over something as silly as an elevator.

chapter 9

I N THE FORTY hours each week that Cynthia did spend in the office, she was living a second life. She was still the wife of Timothy and eager to share the tales of their house shopping and ambitions for a lavish lifestyle, but she was also engaged in a dangerous flirtation. While she was certain that Timothy treated her right and that they were completely content in their marriage, some part of her heart longed for a fresh romance. She enjoyed the excitement of being the most beautiful woman in the office. An arbitrary title that was never officially awarded, Cynthia took pride in her status as the 'glamorous' one; the one all the men would stutter around or offer to help, the one all the other women would try to emulate.

Cynthia would appreciate and delight in each subtle advance and compliment from the men in her office. While she outwardly demurred or even flat out rebuked them for these comments, she delighted in the idea that she still had 'the goods.' She was ensuring a follow-up lover should Timothy leave her or die an early death. The rings on her left hand should have made her the hardest to get, but her coy comments and sly winks were almost second nature to her now. She didn't even realize that she was being a flirt most of the time, she was just being Cynthia.

There was one gentleman in particular at work that she dallied about with the most, her counterpart on the accounting team. His name was Erik Chekovich. A tall and well-toned young man, he was at least one year younger than Cynthia, but that was part of the excitement for her. She would dress a little nicer on the days that she would have meetings with him, she would smile a little wider, and be sure to have her hair worn down for extra effect.

He had only recently started with the company, so he was still in the early stages of his infatuation with Cynthia when she had moved to Hurley Pond. They had a bi-weekly meeting to review outstanding invoices and he had made it a habit of refilling his coffee mug, stopping at Cynthia's desk for a few moments of chatting, and offering to escort her to the conference room before their meetings. At first, Cynthia just enjoyed the nervous excitement and the added attention, it felt good to be wanted. But she was always certain to leave the door open whenever they did meet so that no one would suspect anything untoward. It was her own way of making sure things never went further than heated glances and sweet smiles. (Although their coworkers did absolutely suspect an affair given the bits of conversation that they could overhear. They were all certain of it, and while most enjoyed the gossip, a few were genuinely concerned about the damage Cynthia was doing to her own career prospects.)

When Erik and Cynthia would exchange emails, she would add extra little smiley-face icons and would delight when she saw that they were returned. When the accounting team went to lunch, Erik would invite Cynthia along. Usually, she would demur, but it made her happy to know that Erik wanted to spend time with her outside of work. When they had quick exchanges via the inter-office instant messaging system, they would quickly stray into personal conversations regarding their weekend plans, favorite new online videos, and otherwise engage in, what Cynthia called, harmless flirtations.

Cynthia could tell that Erik was certainly attracted to her. Sometimes they would pass in the office and she would catch him stealing a glance at her. Cynthia felt a sense of accomplishment at having merited this man's affections, but wasn't quite sure what to do next. If he made any advances, she would either have to commit to the affair, which would be bad for her personally. The other option was to spurn him at the risk of ruining her professional reputation and making an enemy on the accounting team. She walked this tightrope carefully, and to her credit, it helped to pass the hours quickly as she avoided her work assignments.

Still settling into the new commute and routine, Cynthia left the office that Tuesday in a hurry to get home and continue unpacking. Erik offered to join her as she walked to her car in the parking garage. No danger was suspected or implied in the routine walk to her vehicle, but she still accepted the offer. It was during this little walk that Cynthia's world was thrown a bit off kilter.

"I didn't get a chance to ask you yesterday, but how was your weekend?" Cynthia was shuffling through her purse, looking for the keys to her car. The heavy curls in her brown hair that had been thick and full at the beginning of the day now sat limply against her face, the bright blonde streaks that were supposed to be natural highlights were pulling away from the lock of hair in rebellion.

"It was great. I hung out with some of the guys and then went to dinner with a friend," Erik walked in step with Cynthia up until this point. She stopped in her tracks and continued to search for her keys in her purse. She had found them just a moment ago, but Erik's comment had struck her like an open-palmed slap on the face. Cynthia knew exactly what Erik meant, now she just had to decide how to react. She couldn't really be mad at him for dating, but she also expected him to not say anything. Maybe he had never really been attracted to her at all. Her insecurities began to gnaw at her and she popped her head up with a smile and dangled her keys joyfully.

"Found 'em!"

"Alright!" Erik raised his hand for a high-five but Cynthia was already walking again, markedly avoiding physical contact.

"So, dinner with a friend, eh?" She raised her perfectly threaded eyebrow in an exaggerated manner and let her voice trail off, requesting further explanation.

"Hah, yeah," Erik didn't elaborate any further. It was in that moment that Cynthia realized two things. One was that she didn't know Erik that well at all. She knew him well enough to chat with him at work, but she didn't know who his friends were or how he got on with his parents. She was an intruder in his life just as much as he would be an intruder in hers. The second realization was that he may have only been toying with her as well. She was flooded with regret and shame, even though she had done nothing wrong, she reminded herself once more.

They arrived at Cynthia's car and she excused herself quickly, not wanting to hear any more about Erik's date, or worse, a potential relationship. The entire way home she worried over her actions, was she overly flirtatious and making herself look like a fool in front of everyone? The music on the radio did nothing to soothe her worries as tunes of betrayal and attraction played through her thin speakers.

As she coasted along the highway, she thought she heard a buzz coming from her purse. She looked over and found her phone, missing the fact that she almost sideswiped a car as she careened into another lane.

No messages on her phone, even though she was sure that she heard a buzz. She knew the distinct buzz of her phone because she set it to match the tune of her favorite song. She had absolutely heard it.

She opened her messages and incidentally glanced up at the road to ensure no one was stopping short ahead of her. Cynthia opened up her thread with Timothy and sent him a quick message:

"Driving home now. Can't wait to see you tonight honey!"

She usually never sent these kinds of text messages to Timothy. Their conversations were mostly transactional: "I forgot my travel mug, have you seen it?" "I'll be working late today, sorry to miss dinner again." "I forgot to mention, I have a dentist appointment tomorrow morning. Just got the confirmation call from the doctor."

They weren't much for affectionate messages, or at least they hadn't exchanged many since their wedding. And even then, the sweet little texts had only spiked because of the pre-wedding bliss that they felt because of the immensity of the moment. Most of their darling little notes to each other had been during the courtship phase when they were in college and texting was still a new thing. Once they had settled into the routine of their relationship those messages dwindled and only occasionally resurfaced around anniversaries.

But in that moment of, some undefined anguish over a person she had no feelings for, or at least none that she would admit, she put back on her most reliable accessory, her ability to be a charming wife. It was something that went with every outfit she owned, and surely no one would suggest that it would go out of style. Cynthia treated the things, and the people, in her life as though they were accessories; the added touch to complete the image she wanted to project. At work Erik was the ideal accessory, he complimented her and gave credence to the established fact that she was still desirable. At home, Timothy and their puppy and their furniture were all the accessories that helped her to project the idyllic image that they were living out the American Dream.

Timothy was almost floored when he received the text and was surprisingly overcome with emotion. His wife was really thinking about him. His recent worries over her unenthusiastic demeanor were unfounded perhaps. He saved her message and made a mental note to send her a sweet text too, soon.

chapter **10**

BEFORE MAKING THE assumption that Timothy is the one made to look like a fool because of Cynthia's flirtations, let's take a look at his day. For those who are easily bored by the thought of being cooped up in an office surrounded by mountains of paperwork, ready your pillows, because that was Timothy's workday. After he arrived at work and spent some time looking out at the horizon he would spin back to his desk, hidden under piles of legal documents, file folders, thick packets cinched together with massive binder clips, and a dizzying pattern of post-its shuffled somewhere in between it all.

He would work through lunch and hand over his credit card to the office assistant who would order lunch in for the attorneys. Each of the Lawsons had their own food preferences so they rarely made one large order to split. Henrietta, his glamorous and model-thin cousin, would usually order a salad or wrap from the vegan deli around the corner. Randolph Lawson, Timothy's uncle, would usually order a burger or a Rueben from the traditional deli across the street. The dichotomy of food preferences between father and daughter amused Timothy.

James, his father, would usually order a hoagie and ask for the oil on the side. An action that Timothy knew would appease his mother, if it wasn't for the fact that his father would then dip the sandwich in the oil until it was completely consumed.

Timothy usually requested food from his favorite Chinese takeout place, but would occasionally spring for Pad Thai. On that Tuesday, Henrietta knocked on the door to his office and placed his lunch and credit card on the flattest pile she could find on his desk. She cleared a little corner for herself and began to dress the salad that she had ordered.

This was an occasional treat for Timothy to have his cousin join him. Not only were they lifelong friends, but they had a quick repartee like brother-and-sister without all the baggage of sibling rivalry. Timothy inquired about Henrietta's case work and they chatted back and forth a bit about upcoming deadlines for filings and pouring through depositions.

Timothy was working on a case where he would be representing the Hydroline Corporation. The one with all the commercials that just show beautiful sunsets, but that don't ever say exactly what they do. Well, Timothy had to read through what they actually do and it was not pretty. The company operates in multiple countries, but the global headquarters were located right in their city. The majority of the Hydroline business was in mining minerals from the ground to be used in fertilizers and other byproducts. It would leave the soil where they were mining completely depleted of any nutrients. They had legally acquired the land, which otherwise would have gone undeveloped, but now they were being sued by a local community claiming that Hydroline had misled the municipality and had not explained the potential negative repercussions of their mining.

The Lawson firm had started out fighting the big companies that were polluting the environment, and now Timothy was preparing to defend one of them. The corporate lifecycle had come full circle- they had officially sold out.

But this was to Timothy's benefit. He had calculated that based on the mortgage payment, the homeowner's insurance, the extended commute, and the remaining amount left on his car loans that he would need to work extra hours for the next three years straight. This wasn't even accounting for his student loans, which he knew he could ask his father to help with, but he preferred to not employ that option. This didn't take into account Cynthia's car payments and student loans. He tried not to worry her about their finances since she was also so insecure about making less than him. But between the two of them, there was a lot to worry about. At least the Hydroline case would keep him well paid for a while so that they could get their payments in.

(Yes, if you have done the mental calculations correct, they had three car payments between the two of them. Timothy had totaled a car when he was still in law school and owed more on it than it was worth. He paid down what he could from the check from his insurance company but it left him without enough to eliminate the car loan or buy a new car, so he took out a second car loan. It was the only way that he could buy the newest model of the car that he had been driving. Austerity had never been a concept he wanted to familiarize himself with.)

Henrietta could sense that Timothy was stressed so she tried a few different topics to see if she could get her older cousin to relax a bit. "You know, a salad every once in a while, might be a good idea."

"Nah, I love the way sesame chicken tastes, you know, it has flavor, whereas kale tastes like nothing," Timothy shoveled a forkful of rice and chicken into his mouth.

"Kale is actually kind of bitter, it's very strong."

"You're not selling me on it."

"Okay, I'm just saying that you've been working around the clock, only eating take out. You're not twenty-one anymore. You should start to care for your body a little bit so that you can enjoy your retirement."

"That's a long way from now," Timothy sighed.

"Yes, but if you build healthy habits now it will be easy to maintain."

He appreciated Henrietta's concern. Cynthia would comment from time to time that she thought she was getting pudgy, but Timothy never knew what to say to that. Should he disagree with her, but be supportive of any efforts to eat healthily or exercise? He had certainly funded enough of her shopping in that department.

At least once every few months Cynthia would find some new cure-all diet or workout fad that would make her skinny again without having to give up brownies or potato chips. Usually, she would purchase all of the necessary items (new weights, protein shakes, mixers, prepackaged meals, new workout gear) and commit to the plan for one week. Then the weekend would come and she would want to reward herself for her hard work with wine and chocolate and steak. Then she never picked it back up on Monday.

Cynthia often joked aloud that she loved her curves. She loved her full body. She loved herself and at her size, there was more to love. Each was a slight against herself, a joke at her own expense. But truly, Cynthia loved nothing about herself. If she loved her body and the cells and veins and tendons within it, she would have been better hydrated, eaten lean foods and nuts, and stopped polluting her body with excessive sugar. Just judging by her diet and lack of exercise, she actually hated herself so much that she was chasing a slow and painful death. Don't worry though, Cynthia's actual demise will be much sooner than she could have ever expected, and completely unavoidable at this point in our tale.

Timothy noticed a tire starting to form around his gut so he had started to wake up early and visit the gym in their apartment complex each morning. Cynthia only noticed once or twice that he had left, but never asked where he had been. He had been able to get into a good routine and had been starting to do some serious dead-lifts when they purchased the house on Hurley Pond. For a few months, Timothy had been able to shed pounds and add muscle definition. He was proud of his burgeoning biceps and his just-now-noticeable abs. During the few moments that he was naked in front of Cynthia for their bi-weekly consummations, she didn't seem to notice or comment on his improving physique. He had even gone so far as to point out that the sleeves on his shirts felt tight. Cynthia didn't take the hint. With the move to the new house, and no encouragement from his wife, he stopped abruptly. He no longer had access to the community gym at the apartment complex. He could have looked into the gym facilities on the first floor of the office building, but that would be an additional monthly cost that he wasn't sure he could afford.

No matter, Henrietta put on her finest southern belle charm and changed the topic after spearing a carrot with her plastic fork.

"So, when do I get to see this new dream home that you and Cynthia have found?"

"Uh, well it's kind of a mess right now," Timothy garbled his words.

"Oh, I figured that, but once you're all settled in and cleaned up, don't you plan on having us all over for a house-warming?" Henrietta wiped her mouth with her paper napkin to signal that she was done with her meal.

"Probably, we haven't gotten that far yet." Timothy was a terrible liar. Cynthia had been asking Timothy for a house-warming party. Luckily the weather was forecasted to stay nice and temperate so he suggested a barbecue with their close friends. Cynthia protested explaining her desire for a Great Gatsby style soiree. Timothy explained how impossible it would be to execute on such short notice. Cynthia conceded on the condition that they have a New Year's Eve party under said theme. She loved The Great Gatsby and that whole era. Or, more specifically, she loved the movie and the costumes and the glamor. She hadn't read the book at all, if she had, perhaps she would have realized the caution against the disillusionment of the American Dream. But, Cynthia preferred movies over books any day.

Given that both her attempted topics failed, Henrietta excused herself. She also excused Timothy for not inquiring about her own personal life. Her recent divorce was still dragging on her mentally and the deep bags that had developed under her eyes had aged her flawless face in a matter of months. Timothy never asked how she was handling it.

Maybe it was that he thought it wasn't his business, but he had never shied away from any topics in the past. *Maybe he is afraid that he will start to entertain the idea of getting one himself.* Henrietta regretted the thought immediately, but she didn't dismiss it. Timothy never seemed particularly happy with Cynthia, although her own poor opinion of her cousin-in-law could have clouded that assessment. Henrietta always regarded Cynthia as being very shallow, which wasn't necessarily untrue, but it made it difficult for the two women to have any conversation that wasn't terribly stunted and inorganic. She just couldn't find much to relate to, and then once she became separated, and then divorced, Cynthia treated Henrietta with an entitled disdain. It didn't matter that Cynthia treated Timothy like he was just another piece of furniture, she was still married and could, therefore, talk down to or just flat out ignore Henrietta.

The leggy blonde sat back down to her own stack of paperwork on her desk and jumped online to see if she had any new messages on any of the six dating websites that she was subscribed to. Nothing new today, but Henrietta remained hopeful. She had been on a few good first dates recently, but wasn't satisfied with biding her time waiting for an invitation to go out again. She grabbed her phone and texted her most recent date to see if he wanted to grab drinks after work.

There, that made her feel better, more in control of her own future.

As the work hours flew by Timothy continued to pour over documents related to scientific measurements of ground soil and moisture and sediment and many other things that he had no clue about. After re-reading the definition for "ground cover collapse" for what felt like the millionth time he looked up and realized that the sun had set and he was the only one left in the office. He texted Cynthia to let her know it would be another late night for him. She responded back quickly reminding him that she was out with Bentley for his doggie spa treatments so she was going to be home late as well. They agreed to eat dinner separately and ended their conversation. At least Cynthia sent a "<3" so it could be implied that she meant to say "I love you," but it was just a little emoji heart and it could have meant anything.

With his mind already off of work, he strolled across the street to Cheap Eats, a local sports bar that catered to the after-hours crew. Timothy had been going there more and more often as his caseload increased. He knew the exact order that he wanted: a bacon cheeseburger with tater tots. It was an easy enough meal and one that he was likely paying way too much for, but he was hungry and overworked. The cortisol levels in his bloodstream demanded red meat and fat.

He sat down at the bar to order, not planning to stay any longer than necessary. The bartender who was there almost every time he had visited in the past few months was working that evening. She spotted him as he walked in and waved. After she finished pouring a fresh beer for another customer she walked over to where Timothy was perched by the end of the bar. "Hey stranger!" She flashed a brilliant smile that went perfectly with her silky blonde hair and tanned features. She looked like you would expect an attractive young bartender to look, and she was friendly, working hard for her tips.

"Hi," Timothy made eye contact very briefly before looking away. "Can I get my usual order to go?"

"Sure thing," she smiled and walked over to the computer behind the bar to punch in his order. He caught some score updates on one of the big screens as he waited and thought about texting Cynthia again, but he wasn't sure what to say. He could tell her about his day when he got home.

The sports news had distracted him well enough. Before he knew it, the bartender was walking back over with his order in a to-go bag. She also set down a Styrofoam cup and straw. "You never order anything to drink with your meal, I'm throwing in a cola on the house, ok?" She smiled as she added some napkins and a straw to the bag.

"Thanks, I really appreciate that." Timothy grabbed the bag and cup and smiled again, not sure if he should say anything else.

"Of course, sweetie. And next time, just text me when you're coming in, I'll have your order all set for you." She must have made this offer to all of the regulars, right? Surely a method to secure that she would be the one to submit their order and get credit for the sale.

"Oh, yeah, that would be awesome." Timothy put the bag back down so that he could grab his phone. He punched in her number, sent a test-text, and said good evening.

By the time he made it across the street to his office he saw that he had a new text message waiting for him. "Always great to see you. Come again ;) -KellyAnne"

The winking face caught him off guard. Again, he reassured himself that she was just being nice. But what if she was flirting? Certainly, he wasn't trying to encourage her. Although, it was nice to know that some woman was trying to get his attention in *that* way. He let the thought marinate in his mind as he devoured his meal. He assured himself that he would never cross any line, but was proud that he still had the physical charms to catch someone's eye (potentially, maybe, probably not.)

chapter **11**

A FTER RETURNING HOME on that Tuesday evening, Cynthia draped herself across their plush couch and reclined with a glass of wine. She had an idea to fix dinner for herself, but she couldn't decide what to whip together so she scrolled and scrolled through the internet while her favorite dating show replayed on the large-screen television.

Bentley was comfortably napping on his dog bed. After his monthly appointment for hair and shampoo service, he was usually very tired. He also had a nail detailing on that particular evening and the monthly subscription of mail-order dog treats had arrived. Bentley was certainly living the high life.

After perusing the regular websites that she enjoyed and exhausting the latest celebrity gossip news, Cynthia glanced over at the stack of boxes in the hall that still needed to be put away. She wanted the house to look perfect so that she could invite friends over for a dinner. First, she needed to make sure all the painting was finished before she moved all of the little items into the rooms. And before that could be done, she needed to confirm the colors with Timothy, and that, of course, required them to speak to one another, which was becoming more and more infrequent.

As she dwelled on how little she knew about Timothy's day or week and felt the first numbing thoughts of loneliness, she glanced up at the television screen to see a charitable commercial playing. Children in tattered clothing, caked in dirt, were smiling up at the camera, looking happy but still hopeless. Her misdirected anger made her want to groan aloud in her empty house. "Why do they always show these sad commercials, like anyone *here* can make a difference?"

The next channel was showing a news segment, "how to spot the terrorist next door." Listening for a few moments Cynthia nodded along, trying to memorize the warning signs that the experts were presenting. She would have to be on the lookout for radical behavior, people who denounced the American way. She would be a good little citizen and report anything if her suspicions were aroused. The segment ended and she turned off the television and let the remote hit the coffee table with a loud thud. Pampered Bentley popped up from his doggie-bed, alarmed by the sudden noise in the otherwise quiet house.

After a moment, she turned her attention back to her computer and spent some time searching for jobs. Cynthia Lawson was a junior account executive at a marketing firm assigned to CPG - consumer packaged goods. She worked to sell homemakers more laundry detergent after telling them that only bad moms let their kids go to soccer practice in dirty trainers. She told men in the throes of a mid-life crisis that they could buy success if they bought the newest grill and outdoor gear. She told insecure singles to purchase only the finest perfumes and colognes because if they didn't smell right, they would be alone forever.

Her job was to understand the insecurities of the consumer and appeal to their natural fears. She did her job in an average and perfunctory manner. Some months the clients were happy, other months they were mad. Cynthia relied on the standard excuse, "you can't make people buy something they don't want." But people were always buying things they didn't need or want. Cynthia just never put in the extra effort to really sell any of the products. She could have made those faceless and anonymous consumers buy. If she would have just been a bit more convincing in her ad copy, the consumers might have always said "yes!"

All of Cynthia's coworkers were doing just that. Cynthia never faced her own 50/50 success. She believed that she was a star on the team and that the bad months were beyond her control and beneath her level of experience. She was vying for a promotion. Cynthia had dropped significant hints to her boss and hinted at a promotion to the ladies who sat nearby. If enough people gossiped about the promotion and believed it was happening, then it would happen. Cynthia believed that generating buzz would be sufficient to elevate her in the eyes of her superiors. She also believed that all attention was good attention because, after all, it was being spent on her.

That evening she searched for jobs with "senior" in the title, that would offer at least $10,000 more a year than she was currently making. She figured if she could get a counter-offer, she could leverage for more money. It seemed to make sense, although nothing she saw stood out as very glamorous. She couldn't write into her high school reunion that she was working for some low-level shipping company or an organization that handled financial services products.

She saved a few job postings on her computer before finally logging off, shutting down, and fixing herself a bowl of ice cream. It was too late to eat a heavy meal, and she had a long day. Besides, when Timothy wasn't home for dinner she could cheat a little on her diet. The words as they formed in her mind struck her immediately. *Shut up!* She scolded her own mind. She wasn't on a diet and hadn't been for months. But the word "diet" isn't what jarred her. It was the word "cheat," because she knew deep down that what she was doing each day was crossing the line, and that if she ever had to explain herself to Timothy, there was no other way to explain what she was doing, flirting with Erik.

She devoured her ice cream and polished off the bottle of wine that she had opened earlier in the week. She waltzed into the kitchen feeling a gentle buzz and washed up her dishes and silverware. With nothing better to do, she elected to go into the stack of boxes in the front room and start unpacking the little knick-knacks and baubles that still had to be placed around the house.

That was when an enormous force stopped her in her tracks. Sauntering onto her thick tile floors, trying to escape through the kitchen and out through the garage was an enormous cockroach.

Her screams startled Bentley who began to bark immediately. Frozen in his tracks, the invader remained still, taunting Cynthia with his presence. She very bravely ran around the other side of the kitchen island, through the living room and up the stairs. She swiped her phone on the way up and called Timothy. At this point, her hysterical tears were drowning out the words she left on his voice mail. She would never be able to sleep soundly in that house, ever. They would need to back out of the sale. They could not stay here if such an infestation existed.

Wretched roach. Wretched roach. She found herself muttering it aloud as she frantically waited for Timothy to return. Too afraid to go into the bedroom to hide and risk seeing one up there she loitered on the lower steps peering around the corner for movement in the kitchen.

By the time Timothy had arrived Cynthia was slightly calmer. Her breathing was normal, but her eyes reflected the internal anguish she was feeling. Resigned, he knew he wouldn't get a sound night's sleep without first giving Cynthia a sleeping pill. Although those often made her cockroach-infested nightmares all the more graphic and traumatizing.

After assuring her that he would take care of *it*, he checked the kitchen, only to see that it was completely empty. Not a bug in sight. He ripped off a paper towel from the stand on the counter, mimed the action of stooping low to capture and kill the bug, and then proceeded to the garage to throw the empty paper towel in the trash can. Maybe that bit of acting would spare Cynthia some night-terrors, and secure them both a good night of sleep. She hugged and thanked him as they made their way upstairs. A moment that brought them back together ever so slightly.

chapter **12**

UNTIL, THAT IS, the phone rang at the inconvenient and terrifying hour of 2 AM. A phone call at that time could only bring ominous news. A death, a stroke, an accident of some kind. The news, conveyed to Timothy Lawson by the local police, was that his cousin, Henrietta, had been arrested and she was requesting that he come down to the local jail to pick her up and pay her bond.

Throwing on his jeans as quickly as he could, he sped down to the address that he was given, oblivious to the irony of his own speeding on the way to a police station. He filled out the required paperwork and began to ask questions of the officer behind the desk. He knew that his cousin would know everything that he did about protecting her own rights, but he still felt the need to ask. Even though they weren't siblings, they had always functioned as such for each other. And now, his cousin, his pseudo-sister, was in trouble.

He hadn't inquired about the charge or why she was brought in. He knew he would hear that story soon enough. After several long minutes pacing and scrolling through his social feed, seeing the idle updates from the loners and night owls, keen to share every thought that came into their mind in the late hours of each evening, Henrietta appeared through the beige door. She stood there silently, awaiting some kind of reaction from Timothy, but his thoughts were too slow to process as the door clicked shut with a resounding metal _thunk_.

Her face was swollen and her shirt was ripped, her hair was fraying out like a halo, incapable of being restrained by the loose elastic trying to force it into a pony-tail. The beautiful blonde that he had always seen as so polished and put together was in shambles before him.

Timothy motioned for her to follow him and they silently made their way to his vehicle. Both buckled in, he drove the speed limit the entire way back to his house. Henri would stay the evening on the downstairs couch and he would drop her at her downtown apartment in the morning before work. This hadn't been discussed, Timothy had decided and Henri didn't ask or object so it was just settled, wordlessly.

As they neared the entrance to his new home, Henri finally broke the silence, an unseen force becoming stronger and stronger with each passing mile.

"This neighborhood looks nice," she mumbled as she stared at her own dark reflection in the passenger window, her forehead pressed against the cool glass.

"It is," Timothy agreed. Not sure how to proceed.

"I'm sorry that this is my first time seeing it, your new house."

"Well," Timothy shrugged as they pulled into the driveway. No lights were on in any of the other houses except for the upstairs front window of his own home.

Henri started to unbuckle her belt, which suddenly made Timothy irrationally angry. "Hold on!" he scolded her, moving his arm to catch her wrist. "You have got to tell me what happened."

Henri fumbled for words, unsure of where to start or how to break it down to its most basic forms. "I was drunk."

After a long pause, Timothy prompted her to continue. "My latest e-boyfriend, e-connection, whatever hasn't spoken to me in a few weeks. Another rejection. Another failure. I decided to self-soothe with some wine and a movie to celebrate my single life." She flippantly tossed her hands at the term, showing her disdain for the situation she had found herself in. Timothy stayed quiet to let her continue.

"As I started to feel worse and pity myself more, I drank some more. And then," she paused for effect, "I went online and started just flipping through updates." She gasped loudly and her pale face turned a harsh pink, her eyes welling up. "And then I saw that *he* is engaged. To *her!*" The emphasis on both pronouns told Timothy exactly who the 'he' and 'her' were. Henrietta's cheating ex-husband and the hussy who he did the sleeping around with. He reached out an arm to try and comfort her, she moved her arm to swipe her eyes.

"So, in my drunk and pathetic state, I decided to pay them a little visit. But I was pulled over before I could even get there. So, I guess even though I'll be facing a DUI, I'm not also facing the worst humiliation of my life." Henri offered a weak smile as she concluded her story. Timothy didn't know what to say or how to comfort her. The situation that she was in was truly heinous, but she had been responsible for it all.

He climbed out of the car and she followed suit. A stack of blankets and pillows was left out on the couch in the living room by Cynthia, who had long since retreated to the comforts of their bedroom. "The guest room isn't set up yet," Timothy apologized, although at that hour any place to sleep that wasn't a jail cell was just fine for Henri.

"That's okay," she whispered. Timothy poured her a glass of water and left it on the coffee table. Bentley had sleepily climbed from his doggie bed next to the television into Henri's lap. Unable to fight his instinct to inspect every new entrant to the house, he sleepily yawned as he fell back asleep. Henri smiled and pet him for a bit.

"I'll see you in the morning," Timothy whispered, not wanting to wake Cynthia or continue their conversation in the house. Cynthia had never warmed to Henri and this incident was sure to add fuel to her fire. Where others might have been empathetic or politely pitied her, he expected Cynthia to offer visible spite and increased hostility towards his cousin.

As he crawled into bed, Cynthia rolled over to ask if everything was ok. He told her it was and that they would talk about it in the morning. Accepting his response, she rolled back over and quickly fell back into sleep. But Timothy stared at the ceiling, willing sleep to descend upon him, but it stood him up like a bad prom date.

His mind tossed over the facts of Henri's recent downfall. Her marriage wasn't broken like an object that was shattered in one instant. There was no accident, no loud clang of ceramic on the floor, no 'who did this', no rush to clean it up and repair it. Their marriage had been dismantled, systematically undone, each small part and piece was taken away, observed, and hidden in a remote location to ensure that the pieces were never assembled again. Her ex-husband's affair might have been the final straw or the easy explanation, but they had drifted apart, non-verbal and uncompromising for too long.

Puzzled over his own concern about Henri, he wondered for a quick moment if something like that could happen to him and Cynthia. Could that be them in just a few years or just a few months? Were they already slipping away from each other, were strong currents moving them further apart with each moment?

PART 2

Ambition

"We're trying to bring you the latest information. Our crew has been pushed further back from the blast zone. They no longer have any view of the house." The seasoned female anchor on the local evening news trailed off, unable to convey any additional information. At least, no more than they'd repeated multiple times in that segment. Her stern voice, amplified and modulated, was unable to provide the people of her community with the answers that they wanted.

"You mean where the house once stood," her co-anchor corrected her. An older gentleman who was several years overdue for retirement, he seemed to delight in finding any small fault with her reporting. She was able to hide her disdain for his nit-picking again, which was good, since the cameras were focused on her face in close-up. There were no live images to show that had any relevance to the developing story. They could play that amateur video again, but it was only thirty seconds long. They both moved on to other topics as per the script on the monitors in front of them.

chapter **13**

AFTER TWO ROUNDS of "which date works for you?" the Lawsons and the Ryechiks were able to decide on an evening to have dinner together. Having only been in the house for a few weeks, the Lawsons hadn't ventured out much to meet any of their neighbors. As they prepared to walk over to the Ryechik's house that Friday evening, they commented to one another that they would need to make an effort.

Knowing that the grass needed trimming, the cars needed washing, and the flower bed needed to be redone, it seemed that there would be a lot of opportunity coming up that weekend for them to be out and about, to see and be seen. Timothy would surely need to ask Dan, he confirmed the man's name with Cynthia again, for help with getting the new lawnmower started. Timothy had not called the lawn services that his wife had researched, leaving their lawn an embarrassing mess for several weeks.

Cynthia planned to ask the old lady who lived across the street, Mrs. Schor for some advice on how to best fertilize the hydrangeas she would plant. The Lawsons had a plan for how they would be able to make friends with their closest neighbors. Cynthia dreamed of popular backyard barbecues through the summer where everyone would marvel at how the house was decorated and how lucky they were to have a view of the pond from their backyard.

At 503 Hurley Pond, there were a very different set of preparations taking place. While most people would make a point to "tidy up", the Ryechiks were mussing up their home. With only a few pieces of furniture throughout the first floor, Melinda had to make use of every decoration and throw pillow that she could find to make the space looked "lived in." She marched blankets and books down the stairs, emptying out their bedroom and casting items about as though they were always in use. By six that evening the entire second floor was empty, save for the Ryechik's bed, and the entire first floor looked fairly normal. There were end tables and some pictures on the mantle.

The Ryechiks had disposed of most of their possessions over the previous months. Knowing that most people expect to see a home that is furnished. It still looked a little bare when the Lawsons arrived, but she figured it would pass, maybe they would assume that she had been organizing too much in preparation for their visit.

"Oh hello!" Melinda remarked as she opened the door. "We thought you would just walk on through the back."

Cynthia and Timothy tried to hide their surprise at such a comment. Surely, they weren't *that* familiar with their neighbors yet. Melinda was confused by Cynthia's outfit. She was in a tight-fitting black dress, more appropriate for a cocktail party than a casual dinner. Timothy was dressed in jeans and a polo, so he seemed to understand what was appropriate to wear. Cynthia either didn't notice what he was wearing and therefore couldn't take any cues from her husband, or she simply wanted to make an added effort to impress the Ryechiks.

The truth was that Cynthia simply had to be the most beautiful person in any room, having already seen Melinda in person she wanted to employ every trick she knew. Cynthia styled her hair and put on her special evening make-up as well as tear drop diamond earrings with a matching necklace and bracelet. She didn't think that she could be overdressed.

And her plan worked in some ways. Melinda felt a little underdressed in her house jeans with one of Jack's flannel shirts draped over her white tank top. After a busy day at her own job and hurrying to fix up the house for guests, she didn't have much time to fuss over her looks, not that she ever spent much time primping herself.

Unaware of the subtle war of the wardrobes going on in front of him, Timothy asked where he should put the beers that he brought to share with Jack. Cynthia asked the same for the wine that she brought. The Lawsons were part of a club that afforded them access to the best wines in the state and regular meals at the club restaurant. Cynthia had recently started the monthly subscription with the club and had been receiving a new package of four bottles of wine each month. She brought one white and one red with her that evening, not knowing what her neighbors would prefer.

After exhausting the topic of how the Lawsons were settling in, the couples exchanged information on their day jobs, their alma maters, and their plans for the summer.

Much as fictional vampires must practice the motions of breathing and the human tendency to fidget, the Ryechiks had to practice agreeing to common place comments and nodding or smiling on cue at pop-culture related jokes.

Immediately, the Lawsons could sense that there was something off about the Ryechiks. Timothy figured he was just exhausted from another long week. He was trying very hard to continue the conversation and assumed that the asymmetry was due to his attempts to overcompensate for his low energy. Cynthia had her antennae up however; she didn't like how off-kilter the night felt. The house was too clean; the discussion didn't flow the way she would have expected it to. When Timothy and Cynthia had met their other neighbors, Dan and Caroline, they clicked instantly. The dinner with the Ryechiks felt forced.

And it should have felt off, in reality, these two couples shared very little in common with the exception of their street address. The Ryechiks were two rogue Americans trying to make a statement profound enough to spark change, to inspire others to action. They were actively pursuing methods and publishing materials speaking out against and seeking to undermine the easiest targets in American society: greed, ignorance, waste. They were on no watch list, no agency knew what they were about to do, but they were mere weeks away from, excuse the crude metaphor, pulling the trigger.

The Ryechiks were principled, a stark contrast to their neighbors who appeared to be on the same hamster wheel that everyone else was on. For the Ryechiks, they couldn't comprehend an existence like the one the Lawsons were living. After just a small bit of conversation, they realized just how wide a chasm was that existed between where each couple stood ideologically.

For Jack and Melinda, the evening was carefully constructed, not letting anything slip. Their nearly empty home, that had been staged for the evening, was the perfect metaphor for the final stages of their plan: a shell, a strategically placed impression, a well-hidden identity.

Timothy and Cynthia spent most of the evening providing details of their wedding and honeymoon and how excited they were to move into the neighborhood. Jack asked well-timed questions to prompt the Lawsons to continue talking, they seemed content to boast about their lavish ceremony and vacations so he let them do just that. Melinda followed Jack's lead and because their neighbors were so thrilled to have an audience, they didn't much notice how little the Ryechiks were saying at all.

The quartet moved from the patio to the dining room as the meal was ready. After drinks were poured and plates of food constructed, the conversation turned to the time-honored question of "so, what do you do?" Quick to impress others while simultaneously bemoaning how un-appreciated she was at work, Cynthia answered first. After her quick, but well-rehearsed answer with her parroted, trumped-up, workplace jargon, Jack furrowed his eyebrows.

"No, no. I don't mean what do you do for money. What do you do with your free time? What do you enjoy doing?"

"Oh," Cynthia paused a moment to absorb the shock of the direct question. She mulled it over, sure that any answer she could think of would not be satisfactory. She had the feeling that she was being appraised, ex-amined. She didn't feel up to the test. "Well, I take care of my dog, and I read, and I watch television. I really like Dating Dilemma." Cynthia ref-erenced a show that involved hidden cameras and one member of a couple being duped by paid actors into cheating on their significant other as they sit and watch the live feed of the cameras in a sound booth. Some resist the advances and get the prize money, but the ratings always soar when the person being duped admits that they don't really love their partner or make the first move and kiss someone else. A truly repulsive concept, but the high ratings kept it on television each season.

Melinda couldn't help but let out a little laugh. She and Jack would usually mock those dramatic shows when they saw a commercial or ad. "Sorry," she blushed when she realized that she had in fact offended Cynthia.

"It's kind of silly. I'm always cheering for the couples to stay together, but I find the drama to be kind of entertaining. I get stressed at work, it's nice to watch something and realize that my life is not nearly that bad."

Timothy laughed along, "It better not be anything like that, I don't want to see some grainy video of a guy hitting on you." Cynthia didn't smile as big at this comment as her mind tried to figure out if the parking garage at work did have cameras and if there was actually any video evidence of Erik flirting with her.

Before Jack could chime in with his personal thoughts on the show and its potential negative impact on those watching it, a flurry of chimes and buzzes went off. Each of their cell phones called out in unison, "look at me, look at me." Had it just been one person's phone it might have gone ignored until the evening had concluded. However, it was so unlikely that they would all receive a different notification at once, it had to be some system generated alert. Melinda stood and walked over to the corner of the kitchen island where her phone was charging. Cynthia and Timothy were already drawing their phones from their pockets and unlocking their screens.

"Oh no," Cynthia drew her hand to her mouth.

"There was a bombing down in Sarasota," Timothy read out the information that he could process.

"Sarasota?" Jack asked as he stood to retrieve his own phone from the coffee table where he had left it.

Melinda was reading the notification on her own phone. "It looks like they already think it was terrorism."

The four were now entranced in the notifications that were coming in. A perfectly nice evening marred by violence, how quintessentially American. As they read out the latest headlines to one another, their phones began to chime independently. Social connections were checking in online to let people know that they were unharmed.

"Mark and Tammy are OK!" Melinda read out, directing her comment towards Jack who had been silently scrolling and typing into his phone since the news broke. He visibly sighed and let his shoulders drop.

"Thank goodness," Jack crossed the room to sit next to Melinda.

"They're our good friends, we just saw them last weekend." Melinda explained to Cynthia and Timothy. "I feel so guilty that I am relieved that they are okay. Someone's friends or family has been killed. I shouldn't feel good about knowing that our friends are okay." Jack soothed her by rubbing her shoulders.

"It's so senseless," Cynthia offered, letting her thoughts escape.

"There has got to be some way to stop all of these attacks. They aren't every day, but it is still too often." Timothy added. "Why do they hate us so much? Why do they want to kill us so much?" he added on.

Jack sifted through the thoughts going through his mind. Who do you mean by *they*? Was he assuming it must be some middle-eastern extremist group? And if it is, he should know why they would hate us. We're causing the environmental shifts that are leading them to starvation and forced migration to violent cities. We're turning our backs to them when *they* need asylum. We have shows dedicated to our 4,000 square foot houses and how much food we can binge eat in one sitting, but yet we have no room and no resources to help.

He kept those thoughts in. Instead, he offered an alternative.

"Honestly, if any smart terrorist wanted to take more Americans out, they would open up a few popular fast-food franchises,"

Melinda moved her hand slightly to touch his arm.

"No, it's true. They could keep killing us all slowly the way that we have been killing ourselves for decades." The puzzled look on Cynthia and Timothy's face didn't deter him. "Yeah, maybe open up a cell phone store too, keep handing out these little blocks of technology that we can't pry our eyes away from for the ten minutes it takes to drive home. Just let us gorge ourselves on cheap food that will give us heart disease and diabetes. Let us kill each other because we can't bother to pay attention while we drive. Then they can wipe their hands clean of any responsibility. Just like the big corporations do. 'Oh, it's not our fault that people consume our products, they should know to only have that much sugar in limited quantities.' It's bull. It's sanctioned murder and it already happens every day. This attack tonight just sped up the process for a few people who might have still had time to make the right choices in their lives. But yes, let's get all up in arms about how we can stop people from going online and learning how to build a dirty bomb. That'll save another dozen lives this year, but let's ignore the fact that our entire country is being pumped full of chemicals and additives and that our government looks the other way because the companies that make that junk are paying politicians to keep the status quo!"

Jack's face was red, his neck was tense and one of the veins on his neck was throbbing. "Honey," Melinda whispered.

"Sorry," he shook his head and seemed to snap out of whatever mindset he was in, or perhaps he was just putting his costume back on. "I just get really fired up about this. I mean, I spent ten minutes thinking our friends were hurt, I don't know where my head is at."

"It's alright man. This is what the attackers want us to do, they want us to be afraid and angry." Timothy tried to help diffuse the situation. Cynthia sat quietly with her eyebrows raised and her eyes fixed on Jack. She wasn't sure why, but she was afraid of him and the things that he had just said. Jack excused himself and Melinda asked if anyone wanted more to drink, she hoped her kind smile would ease everyone's tensions just a little bit.

Cynthia tried to nudge her husband under the table to discourage him from accepting another drink. She was ready to leave, especially after Jack's little rant. Besides, she didn't want Timothy to have any performance issues later in the evening. This was the first Friday of the month, which was their special evening, the one of two times each month that Cynthia would allow Timothy to have relations with her.

The Lawsons departed early in the evening. Timothy was a little buzzed and admitted to Cynthia that he liked Jack; he seemed like a man's man. Timothy hoped to be able to actually make a friend, his work schedule permitting. The two men could spend Saturday's grilling and discussing Timothy's plans to construct shelves in the garage.

Cynthia wasn't as impressed, however. "They live in that beautiful house and it looked absolutely empty, isn't that weird to you?"

"I'm sure Melinda just cleaned it up to look nice for us," he assured her. Cynthia would not let her concerns be pushed aside.

"I bet he doesn't even let her decorate, controlling her..." she let her words and their implications hang in the air.

Melinda and Jack were pleased with the evening, but it wasn't anything more than they would have expected. They found it tough to connect with outsiders, with people who were so focused on being normal. They often went through waves of wishing themselves to be more "normal," more like what they were expected to be, and then suddenly being incredibly proud of their status as outsiders.

Perhaps they were best characterized as extremists. Because in their view they were extreme: extreme saving, extreme scrimping, extreme thriftiness, extreme minimalism, extreme anti-materialism. That is an extreme way to live in our society that is all about pushing limits, but is intolerant of anything outside the norm. And Jack had let his own thoughts slip, he worried that he had said too much.

As the pair cleaned up the silverware and the glasses, they discussed their impressions of how the evening went.

"I feel bad for them," Melinda stated as she turned off the warm water and did one final swipe to clean out the suds from the bottom of the sink. "I shouldn't attempt to even judge them, but wow! I mean, they have so much material, so many material items all around them and are so proud of that. But it seemed like there was nothing between them. Nothing connecting them together."

Jack looked at his wife intently, taking in her words. "Maybe they do, and we just didn't see that."

"Hmm, maybe," Melinda shrugged and she dried her hands on a dish towel. "They kept going on and on about their fancy honeymoon, like that is a life achievement."

Trying to determine the root of his wife's frustration Jack asked "should I be taking you on more luxury vacations? Should we forget this plan so that I can shower you with gifts like you deserve?"

Melinda smiled as though she was considering that image, "it could be nice for a day or two, but it wouldn't be us." She kissed him softly.

"Thanks for helping me regain my cool back there," he offered as he wrapped his arms around her waist.

"Of course, once I saw the headline, I knew exactly what you were thinking," she shook her head. He pressed his forehead against hers, willing their minds to connect in some extra-sensory manner. It never worked, but it was a sweet gesture that they exchanged in times of stress.

"So, *our* plan is still on then?"

"You betcha!" she smiled as they passed out of the kitchen and shut off the lights.

chapter **14**

A S WAS USUALLY the case, after an evening with a couple who seemed to be doing just fine, Melinda began to feel the old nagging in her mind. *Why shouldn't I try to dress nicely? Why shouldn't Jack shower me with nice gifts? We can move back our deadline; we don't have to do this.*

This feeling was ingrained in her after a lifetime of feeling like the poor girl. The schools she attended were comprised of mostly kids like her, no one was remarkably rich and no one was exceptionally impoverished. Because of that, the subtle distinctions between upper middle class and lower middle class began to make themselves known. Melinda had grown up in a resolutely lower middle-class home. Her mother didn't make enough to take Melinda out to dinners on her birthday or for special occasions, but they would sometimes have fast food. Melinda never worried where her next meal came from, but she would hear reminders from her mother that she was lucky she had a coupon for a certain item. Melinda only got new shoes when the old ones were worn out. She only ever experienced the excitement of purchasing a "first day of school" outfit when she was in high school and could afford such expenditures with her babysitting money and a part-time paycheck from the local movie theater.

Melinda always felt a little less pretty than the rest of the girls in her class, she felt a little less deserving of the grades she merited, and the scholarships she won to college. She felt a little less at ease when she did go away to school because she knew that she had to keep working hard. After all of that hard work and after all those years between her time as a kid and her current life as a woman who stood on her own, she still felt that nagging in her mind.

So why did she still feel like an outcast? Clothes never new enough, make-up never clean enough, hair never smooth enough. Old insecurities die hard when surrounded by the menagerie of bedazzled and glittering women around her all day. She didn't have intricate highlights in her hair and she didn't wear the newest accessories. These feelings surged after their dinner with the Lawsons. Cynthia was so glamorous and was clearly the superior woman in terms of style. Jack had reassured her worries so many times in the past, but she didn't dare mention them to him now. Not with everything that he had on his mind. How could she bother him with her feelings of inadequacy? She kept quiet about it. By Monday afternoon, Melinda was teeming with self-doubt and insulting each of her own choices.

Before returning from her lunch in the park that day, Melinda took a detour to her favorite coffee shop. She purchased her favorite blend and tossed the receipt. She let the flavor of the coffee saturate her taste-buds, but not without guilt. Was this small, little lie so rotten of her? Only a few dollars spent out of turn, but her caffeine affinity demanded it. Still, she decided not to tell Jack.

Jack hasn't always been so... out of touch. He had the same ambitions that most stable and modest young men had. With his overpriced degree in hand he hoped to earn a living, meet a good woman, marry, start a family and begin ticking off the to-do list of American success very quickly: car, starter home, new car, promotion, etc. But, in a moment where he realized how dull and predictable his life might be, he knew that if he bought all of the things he was supposed to that this life would become an incomprehensible sea of empty decades without additional improvements to make. He began to ask questions again. "Why am I doing this?" "Why am I working here?" "How did we all end up buying the same beige Honda Civic?" He decided to not buy anything (excepting groceries) until he had a sufficient answer. After one month, he purchased a pair of swim trunks. The reason he gave himself was multifaceted: "I want to swim and I would get arrested if I did so naked."

And so, all of Jack's decisions required the same explanation.

"Why am I insisting on the brand name cereal when the store option tastes the same?" If his answer involved status or perception of wealth, he would feel a repulsion that sneaked up into the snarl of his upper lip and then quickly retreated.

And when he finally found Melinda and asked himself, "why do I want to be with her?" his own brain reflexively populated the answer, "because her spirit has been with me all along." It was so deep and profound an answer that he proposed after only two months of dating. The first radical thing that they did together.

How, you might wonder, did the spend-thrift Ryechiks come to own such an opulent house for their tastes? Their home, their house on Hurley Pond, had gone into foreclosure in 2008 along with most of the other homes in the area. The previous owners had put so little down, and then barely scraped together the mortgage payment every month in order to stay in such a home. (Sound familiar?) It was a story all too common with the same common excuses. Hubris, greed, ambition, the American Dream. The Ryechiks didn't enjoy seeing so many others in the throes of financial ruin. In fact, it hardened their resolve to stay on top of their own finances. But they couldn't help but take advantage of the flood of homes that the bank needed to offload.

By the time the bankers came knocking on the door at 503 Hurley Pond, the owners were long gone. They had vacated after punching holes into the house. As if beating it to a pulp would somehow assuage the shame of their financial insolvency. They took violent means as a method for alleviating the anger they felt towards themselves, for buying into the spectacle that was only as solid as dust in the wind.

Because of the state of the house, the bank was quick to offload the property at $50 per square foot. Jack purchased, fixed it up, and invited some of his friends to stay as roommates. They all pitched in for utilities, but Jack paid the laughably small mortgage payment each month by himself. After several years, he had met Melinda and paid off the house. The roommates left and the Ryechiks were very happy for a while.

They both realized that the image of their idyllic life was hallow and empty; just like that house. Costs started to add up as the roof needed to be repaired, and one, then both, bathrooms needed to have the pipes redone. Soon their hearts began to pull them away, not from each other, but from that house. They were being guided to step away, to intentionally break from the pattern. Their plan was born in that moment.

And that was part of why she couldn't tell Jack that she just felt like having a coffee to justify spending those few dollars. Those were dollars that were being taken away from their dream, from the plan. The all-encompassing, looming plan.

For all of the love that she felt for Jack, she worried that she would have one too many moments of feeling the pressure to be perfect and that it would crush her. It didn't happen often, maybe once or twice a year. But she still felt it. She knew that once the plan was in place it would all be better. Everything that they were working for was about to be realized. If some turn of fate forced her to choose between a lifetime of lattes or a lifetime with Jack, she would absolutely choose Jack. But, no one was asking her to make that choice. With the final touches about to be put on the big project he'd been tinkering on for months, their life would never be the same.

It was so close, but because it was so extreme, so far-fetched, it was hard to accept that it was really happening. So, maybe she should savor this latte, how many more opportunities would she have to enjoy one before…

The irony was that as Melinda anguished over her decision to spend $3.50 to treat herself without telling Jack, thus invalidating the data in their budget; Cynthia was a few blocks away in the parking garage with Erik, not having one concern for Timothy, thus invalidating her wedding vows.

Lying in bed that evening, Cynthia looked over at Timothy's back, his body and mind asleep as she was wide awake. Erik had maybe, almost, kissed her that day. There was a moment, the one where you just know it is about to happen, all the barriers have receded to their lowest levels and contact is about to be made. However, a gust of wind whipped the stray news sheets across them, flapping and held in place against Erik's leg. They both looked down, on the way his eye gazed at her ring. The moment evaporated, no, it sublimated, gone into the air. But her cheeks felt hot at the recollection of it. When had Timothy last made her blush? Their wedding day. Maybe?

Cynthia's mind began to invent ways to recreate the scene, to get back to that moment, to see what else could happen. She had only recently started to entertain the idea that she might even be attracted to Erik, she had started to feel that jealousy tug at her when he mentioned having a date, and now a crush was beginning to develop.

But the obstacle still remained: her marriage and the rings that signified it, like handcuffs on her finger binding her to a man who didn't seem to care about giving her what she wanted.

She fiddled and twirled the rings with the tip of her thumb, an expected habit by now. How to keep Erik but not ditch Timothy? Maybe he would die. Too much stress at work, a car accident, something quick. Would Erik run to her side right away, or make her wait the "respectable time" before coming to her? She fantasized about how he might broach the void.

chapter 15

WHILE CYNTHIA WAS very clear again to not cross any lines, she enjoyed the attention that Erik was giving her. He seemed to consistently reach out to her during the workday on the inter-office chat system. He would still ask extra questions about her day and the things that were worrying her: the prospect of a raise or promotion, the chance of rain that would spoil her afternoon lunch at a bistro two blocks away, those kinds of things.

By manufactured chance, they happened to be walking out to lunch at the same time one afternoon and decided to dine together. Cynthia enjoyed the thrill of what might happen if Timothy walked in and saw her there with another man. Surely, he would fly into a rage and demand an answer. Cynthia would claim her innocence; it was just a coincidence (lie). Couldn't he trust her (deflection)? She wondered how Erik would react, would he become defensive and tell Timothy that he ought to take better care of her. The idea that Timothy might not care or that Erik would vehemently deny any affections never occurred to her, she was so sure of her power to keep both men wrapped around her finger.

After lunch, there were no theatrics, they walked back to the office when Erik made a point to change the conversation to his most recent date.

"Oh, another date this past weekend? Aren't you quite the Casanova," Cynthia tried to joke with him.

"Nothing like that, it's actually the same girl from before. I think it's going somewhere." Erik smiled slightly as he walked forward, his head thoroughly in the clouds, unable to see the shocked look on Cynthia's face.

So that lunch out was nothing to him? Maybe just a farewell, it's been nice using you as an emotional crutch. Did he expect her to be happy for him? She wanted to slap him across the face for such a betrayal. But a betrayal of what she didn't want to articulate, and that made her even more angry.

"Cool," was the only terse response that Cynthia could muster.

Erik couldn't figure out why his good news had left Cynthia so frustrated. They rode the elevator up to their office in silence. Cynthia reflexively whipped out her smart phone and began scrolling as a visual cue that she wasn't just ignoring Erik now, she was searching for something else to catch her attention. Erik might have found this rude if he hadn't mirrored her action and started scrolling through himself. Once Cynthia did so, she made it OK for Erik to, the ultimate unspoken rule: I'm done paying attention to you, you can stop pretending to pay attention to me now.

Some people are dying since the day they were born. Others are alive since the day they were born. The difference in meaning is subtle. It would certainly sound good on a bumper sticker or a picture quote on Facebook. Which is how Cynthia let people know who she was. Using quotes from other people that she found to be witty. She scrolled through her feed and found a picture of a mountain reflected in a pristine lake with the word "Live" etched across the image. She reposted it and checked every fifteen minutes on the dot to see how many likes she had and who was conspicuously missing from her list of notifications. That was how she found that exact quote: *Some people are dying since the day they were born. Others are alive since the day they were born.* Too ironic knowing that her days were numbered.

Surely, she would have been even more desperate for a raise had she known the dwindling number of hours she had left to live. Her time was more valuable now that it was in short supply. Since Cynthia did not know about her impending doom, she could not add that onto her pile of reasons that she felt that her effort warranted a raise.

After a day of putting in her usual effort, chatting with the ladies in her cubicle row about whether or not anyone had heard rumors of potential promotions, asserting her dominance as the alpha-female on the team, Cynthia left a few minutes early to make her hair appointment. Every six weeks she had a standing appointment with her 'girl' to touch up her highlights and do a quick trim. When asked, she always accepted the deep conditioning treatment upcharge. The salon was aiming to be a boutique and offered guests chilled colas and snacks, but the soda was always served in a can, not a glass. And the snacks were always in single-serving bags, as though they had been purchased at a wholesale discount store. Still, it was a better-quality experience than the cheapy $15 haircut places that Cynthia swore she would never go to.

Once her $200 bill was paid, Cynthia bounced out to the car, trying to get the air into her freshly styled hair. She felt glamorous and that was the feeling she so longed to cherish. A quick driver's seat selfie and she was on the road to her home, ready to show off her hair to Timothy.

But he wasn't home yet when she arrived, so her post-salon compliments were delayed. The garage bays were empty until Cynthia slid her car into place. The walls were lined with items still to be organized, the list dwindling. She popped over to the mailbox, checking for that monthly statement that she needed to hide quickly. Each time she went to check she always worried that Timothy would pull up at that very moment, his bright headlights illuminating her, flooding light onto her betrayal. Caught in the act. That is what she would be, but that evening he didn't arrive home until much later. By the time he did get home, her excitement had dissipated. Oh well, maybe he'll notice next time.

Flipping through the envelopes as she walked into the house through the garage, she failed to notice that some of the pavers on the front walk were displaced, shifting, moving apart. Could it be something that Cynthia feared, a massive underground hive of cockroaches eating away at the soil beneath their home, burrowing and excavating until the weight of the home couldn't stand on its own for any longer? Or was something else stirring? Could it be innocuous and nothing to worry over, a tree root stretching out a long way from the trunk and popping up a few stones along the way? Maybe. But whatever was coming for her life, she was going to perish with impeccable highlights and no split ends.

That evening the Lawsons ate dinner across from each other. Cynthia checked her phone and Timothy read through a brief. They cleaned their plates separately and Cynthia washed the dishes, leaving them to dry in the rack next to the sink. She retired to the couch and tuned into her Thursday evening television program. She had a favorite show every night of the week. On Thursdays, it was the newest episode of a reality show where people are given the ultimate wedding if they can complete three grueling physical challenges. She poured herself some wine and flipped through magazines during the commercials. Timothy stayed at the dining room table and continued to read until he realized that he was alone. He joined Cynthia on the couch momentarily before excusing himself to take a shower and get to bed early.

A quiet night between two newlyweds may seem normal enough. But young love is supposed to be loud and raucous. It makes noise and cannot be contained because of the sheer force of it. Yet these two young adults had nothing to say to one another, no noise to be made, no force to be reckoned with.

Weren't they doing what they were supposed to do? They were married, an *honest* couple trying to be legitimate in American society. They had gone to college, and still had the student loans to show for it. They had nice cars, European label but assembled in America. They had their beautiful home, they had professional jobs, they had a dog and were planning to have children in a respectable amount of time. How could anybody afford it? How could others seem to make the American Dream work? Maybe they were all drowning in just as much debt as the Lawsons were. If so, then they hid it much better. The pressure was starting to get to them, they were starting to fissure.

In the quiet evening when Cynthia had slipped into bed, Timothy broke the silence with his voice. It sounded like it was coming from someone else, but he was the one to have said it. "What do you want from this life?"

A deep and meaningful question for a late hour, Cynthia responded with ease. "I want everything," she smiled and kissed him on the forehead.

"That's your dream?" he asked in a calm voice. He was truly trying to understand her. He wanted to be able to help support her dreams and then she could support his. But he didn't know what he even wanted out of life.

"Yes," Cynthia responded with a quick shrug of her shoulders and she switched off the bedside lamp.

Oh, Timothy thought to himself in the darkness. A standard answer, how could he give her everything, how could he give himself everything?

chapter **16**

A RRIVING HOME AT a normal hour one afternoon, Timothy
parked in the garage and headed to the curb to perform the usual
ritual. He rolled the over-sized trash bins up the driveway, the large clunky
kind that are picked up with a mechanical arm and must be aligned just-so
to facilitate proper disposal. Then he walked back to grab the mail.

As he surveyed the neighborhood, he did notice one item that was
amiss, a certain something that he hadn't seen before and didn't appear
to belong.

Upon entering his home, he saw his wife hunched over at the kitchen
counter, staring into the glow of her laptop. Assuming that she was sitting
at home surfing the web, he was put out by the fact that she hadn't taken
the initiative to bring up the trash cans or check the mail. He felt slighted,
as though he was just expected to perform these chores without any request
or appreciation from his wife. These thoughts contributed to the rising tide
of spite that he felt towards her, that putrid and corrosive material that can
dissolve even the strongest of bonds.

"Hey," Timothy interrupted Cynthia's job search, she was, in fact,
trying to be productive and not just scanning her social feed as Timothy
assumed. "Did you see that utility vehicle outside?"

Unable to remove her eyes from the screen, "Huh?"

"Yeah, it looked like one of those plumbing or electrical vans, we have
any issues on the block?"

"Not that I noticed." After a beat, Cynthia began to close out of the
application she had started and shut down the device. "Hey don't those
trucks usually say what they do?"

"Yeah, but this one was blank," Timothy had already begun to move about his usual routine of placing his car keys on the peg above the counter.

"Blank? So, like a plain white van?"

"Yeah," Timothy huffed, frustrated that he had to explain what he felt was obvious to his distracted wife multiple times.

"Should we run out and check that no abducted children are being held captive in it?" Timothy laughed at Cynthia's dark joke. She began to assemble the necessary items to prepare dinner. Timothy unfastened his tie and found himself wandering into the front room, what they planned would be a formal dining room but was still empty save for a few boxes. Peering out from the blinds he observed the white van and questioned his own curiosity over it. Parked between the Ryechiks and the house next to them, he could only guess if it belonged to Jack or the next neighbor down. Maybe he did have an uneasy feeling about the van, it was taller and thinner than most utility vehicles, but that was the new style. Shrugging, he retreated from the window and proceeded upstairs to change and avoid idle conversation with his wife. He would need to save that for when they were both seated at dinner.

A few days later, Cynthia began to ruminate more of what had happened to the Mahaskals. She wondered if the mystery van that Timothy had spotted was part of the disappearance of Tyler and Lindsay, the people who once respired, and slept, and interacted within the walls of her home.

She was shocked by her own need to find out where they went. *Did they move into a place that was even better?* That would surely make her feel that their current home was inadequate. *Did they flee the house with no forwarding address because they were criminals, would the FBI show up on their doorstep ready to interrogate the Lawsons for clues?*

Cynthia's overactive imagination was like a playground for all of her worst fears. The previous evening, she had decided to dig out all of the dead plants that lined the front walk. She needed to do some kind of exercise and she figured that rooting around on her hands and knees would be a good hamstring blaster. It certainly was.

As she was ripping out the dried and paper-thin roots of the long-deceased daffodils, a soft voice behind her said: "put your weight into it, dearie!"

Cynthia turned around and guarded her eyes against the sun with her gloved hands. She saw a timid older woman waving from the driveway directly across the street from their house.

"Hello!" Cynthia called out.

The older woman accepted this greeting as an invitation to come over and strike up a conversation. Perhaps she was at home alone all day, or maybe she was just a busy-body in the neighborhood. Either way, Cynthia didn't mind the company.

"Hello there, I'm Lois Schor. I don't think we've been able to meet yet." Cynthia stood and removed her muddied gardening gloves to shake her hand. The women talked idly for several minutes about where the Lawsons were from, how long Mrs. Schor had been in the neighborhood, and the usual niceties.

"Have you had a chance to meet the other neighbors yet?" Mrs. Schor's voice quivered a bit, as would be expected of an octogenarian.

"Yes, I met Dan when we first moved in," Cynthia pointed to the homes of the neighbors as she spoke their names. As though their homes would always contain them, or perhaps that they defined them. Surely in the context of being a neighbor, that is what defined them to her. They lived next to her, across from her, caddy-corner. That was all she knew of them.

"And we had dinner with the Ryechiks just last week."

"Oh, the Ryechiks, how lovely. They were so close to the Mahaskals, I'm sure they really appreciate having another young couple move in next door that they can relate to." Lois smiled sweetly. "Not everyone wants to just pal around with their old-lady neighbor who is always asking for help with her gutters."

Cynthia laughed at her joke. "You know, Dan mentioned that as well," Cynthia wasn't sure how else to respond to Lois' comment. "That the Mahaskals were close to the Ryechiks." Her irritation over the left-over mail began to flare up again.

"Oh yes, they were very close. Always having barbecues together. It seemed like they were always together, back and forth between each other's houses all the time." Cynthia assumed that Lois was exaggerating, but it only made their lack of information on a forwarding address that much more disturbing.

"Really? That's so odd. I have some of the Mahaskal's mail and I wanted to get a forwarding address but the Ryechiks said that they didn't have it."

"Oh, well it's been a couple of months, you could probably pitch it. If it's really important, they'll follow up with them."

Cynthia hated getting the same response on this matter. She was trying to be a responsible homeowner, she wanted to be the kind of person who would go the extra mile to return something. Or in this case, send the mail to a forwarding address. Even she couldn't explain this sick fascination.

"I know, but a couple look like they could be personal correspondence. If it were junk mail, I'd just toss it out, but I would hate to throw away something personal." Liar. Lois didn't catch her passive little lie, but Cynthia was worried that she would be caught. Why even lie about such a thing?

"Oh well. I don't have their address, honey. So sorry. I would have thought that Jack Ryechik would have it, but I guess-" The way that Lois trailed off indicated that there was more.

"What?" a gentle nudge to keep her talking.

"Well, I saw Jack and Tyler arguing one day. I think over some borrowed tool or something because Jack was waving it around. Oh, maybe they were just hollering and having a good ole time. My hearing isn't too good. I don't want to start any neighborhood gossip." That was her exact intention, living by herself with only so much to fill her time with, she longed for a little drama to play out on their street. How could sweet and meddling Mrs. Schor know that a big – B.I.G. – big event was looming on the horizon?

"Well," mirroring her neighbor's tone, inflection, and wording, "like you said they were probably just being a little loud. Men will be men," Cynthia smiled and started to sense that the pace of their conversation was starting to dawdle. "Did you hear anything more about it afterward? If you didn't hear anything then it was probably nothing."

"No, I didn't hear anything about it again, I hadn't really thought of it until now."

"So, it must have been just fine. Too bad for me though, still no clue on the forwarding address."

"Yes. You know, now that I think about it the Mahaskals moved not long after that incident. That was why I didn't have a chance to ask about it."

"Huh," was the only sound Cynthia could make as the gears in her head began to whir.

"You know, I didn't actually see him after that. I saw the moving trucks and the contractors, but not the Mahaskals." Lois Schor looked partially concerned, but also immensely satisfied to have an audience for her fears. Cynthia carried out the rest of the conversation after having changed the topic to the garden. But it didn't stop her from trying to piece this new information together with the eerie feeling that she had about the Ryechiks.

That conversation with Mrs. Schor is what led Cynthia to an afternoon of fervent searching on the internet for Tyler and Lindsey Mahaskal. She checked the local property appraiser website and for any aliases online. She scoured social media and didn't seem to find any particular Tyler or Lindsey Mahaskal with the same town listed in their profile. She wondered what tool it was that Jack had waved at Tyler. Was it a screwdriver or hammer, something small and unremarkable? Or was it a saw or a sledgehammer, something menacing and foreboding? Her imagination was spinning out too many possibilities at once.

And then there was that weird van that Timothy had spotted on their street, potentially the Ryechik's vehicle. She had taken a photo of the van and zoomed in on the license plate after Timothy had gone upstairs the other evening. She ran a search for the plates, but not having any clearance she found nothing except for some basic images on the Mercedes-Benz website of their line of cargo vans. She was proud of herself for not veering into their sedans and SUVs, her car was still relatively new and Cynthia knew that Timothy would never agree to trade in her car for at least another year.

What did all of her conjecture add up to? The Mahaskals were impossible to find, maybe something bad had happened to them. Before she could stop herself, she typed "Jack Ryechik" into the search bar on her computer. She worried that she might find something terrible, perhaps a wanted poster with her neighbor's face staring back at her on the computer screen. She hesitated before clicking "SEARCH."

In that fraction of a second, she heard someone behind her, it was Erik. Flustered that he might see all of the non-work-related tabs open on her desktop, Cynthia quickly locked her home screen before turning back around to face him.

"Hey," her casual greeting sounded overly coy even to her own ears. *Maybe everyone thinks I'm a lousy flirt.* This had never occurred to her before that very moment and it was a thought that would soon be outdone.

"How's it going?" Standing with his hands in his pockets, Erik was all business. He rushed through his sentences without allowing any room for Cynthia to respond, or for himself to breathe. "I wanted to stop by and see if we could just chat now about those monthly numbers. I can't meet later so if there is anything odd or out of place can you let me know? They've been pretty standard over the past few months and probably don't need nearly as much close monitoring."

"Oh," was all that Cynthia could muster. He was canceling their standing meeting. He might as well have just told her, out loud, for everyone to hear, that he was calling off their affair. That ugly word running through Cynthia's mind made her wince. As she replayed that moment in her mind she continued to focus on that physical reaction. She may have never said it out loud, but her brain knew her own motives too well. It was an affair, an intimacy, that she was sharing with Erik, even if their skin never touched.

"Sorry for the short notice," Cynthia read Erik's calm manner as his way of telling her that it was all business. It was only ever business and that she was a foolish overweight wife who was tricked by her own daydreams, once again.

"It's okay, I just haven't had a chance to pull them yet. I can take a look now and I'll shoot you an email if anything stands out." She whipped her chair back around to face her computer, reflexively typing in the code to unlock the home screen.

After a few moments of compiling numbers (she never did run that search on Jack), Cynthia pulled up the internal chat service and pinged Erik.

> C: Hey, the numbers are on track, slightly outperforming last month.

E: Cool, thanks.
C: Anytime. How is everything going?
E: Good. Just have to duck out of here early today
C: Job interview?
E: Nah, date night
C: Wow, getting serious
E: Yep

After a long pause, Cynthia chimed back in. She was grasping at straws, trying to keep Erik's attention. Her need for his affection was beginning to become so obvious that she couldn't hide it from herself anymore.

C: So, when do I get to meet this mystery woman?
E: I guess whenever I get to meet your husband

Too pointed, too direct. What he could have intended to come across in a friendly tone or a passive aggressive remark was emboldened and stripped of all niceties in print. Cynthia chose to ignore the subtext and fairly direct accusation being launched her way. She began to type in a response, but Erik beat her to it.

E: It's not like you would willingly tell Timothy about us being friends
C: There's nothing much to tell
E: Then why not say that you went to lunch with me last week?
C: Because he doesn't control me, I can go to lunch with whoever I want to
E: Okay so he isn't controlling, why not tell him about the wedding loan?

That's right, she told Erik about the loan. The dark secret that she couldn't reveal to her own husband was common knowledge to this other man.

C: I would tell Timothy if he asked flat out
E: Ok so if he asked flat out if you were seeing other men?

C: We're not seeing each other. And the two are totally different. The loan is a lie he wouldn't leave me over. Besides you have a girlfriend, so that's a moot point.

And there it was in black and white, easy for her to read at any time. These were words that she would never have imagined saying out loud. Even though words are just air, contractions of the trachea and voice box. Spoken words are less tangible, Cynthia would have been horrified to hear her own voice speak them. But, those written words, while much more finite were easier for her. She could re-read them, she could imagine a different voice, brusquer and hurtful, uttering them.

Words typed into a box were meaningless to her, disposable, even though there was now no way to get rid of them. They were part of a recorded log of her interactions that was likely being stored in some government warehouse, waiting for the day when it would be used to blackmail her. (Or in this case, until the day that Erik was dragged in for interrogation and accused of rigging the Lawson's house to blow. The suspected motive: an affair. The detectives were able to release Chekovich after his alibi cleared.)

Cynthia went through the rest of that day as if on auto-pilot. She clicked into the correct documents, responded to the necessary emails, and left the office at the correct time. She functioned on pure habit; her limbs knew the correct motions to perform. But Cynthia's brain was otherwise occupied. When had she become this person who was clearly attracted to a man other than her husband? When had she made the choice to be this type of person, someone who hurt people?

She had more freedom than she knew what to do with and a wealth of options that bewildered her. In the presence of so many decisions to make, she elected for the route chosen for her. Chosen by whom? By the media and marketing executives of course! By standard plotlines that only ever reiterated that the greatest thrill after getting married is having an affair and then getting to plan an even better second wedding.

Cynthia drove home that evening, eager to open the new bottle of wine that shipped to their house as part of their monthly delivery service. She and Timothy used to enjoy these together; it was a ritual of a fancy dinner in and their latest bottle to sample. Ever since the move, he was at work all the time. He didn't text her and say, "let's meet here for dinner." He didn't surprise her with take-out. He didn't offer to meet her at happy hour, not that she would have wanted to go anymore.

The last thing she wanted to do was to go to happy hour with her coworkers and see Erik with his new girlfriend. She also didn't want to be hung up talking with her coworkers about their road-trip vacations and perfectly middle-class lives. Cynthia was better than them, she convinced herself. She and her husband lived in a gorgeous house, and would eventually, take that dream vacation, she assured herself as she began to feel her chest tighten. *What if she was just as normal as the rest of them? What if she was terribly and horribly normal and never going to get her fancy trip? What if Timothy would never take her to a nice restaurant again?*

She let out an audible gasp, the ragged kind that sounds like someone who had just breached water for the first time in over a minute, the force of the air hit her lungs as she gasped and tried to steady herself.

She began to breathe a little easier as she turned off the highway and began to follow the familiar roads home. The chain stores that lined the boulevard and slowly gave way to more tree-lined streets and schools eased her back into the reality of her life. Her good life. Cynthia was amazed at her own emotions and how quickly they had taken control of her and with such great force. She had thoughts that, while never articulated or uttered, scared her.

Deciding that she was worried about her marriage and Timothy's recent lack of interest, she decided to cook him a nice meal and save the wine for the two of them to share. She now had a plan to get everything back on track. Starting today. Starting right now.

As she pulled onto Hurley Pond, she spotted Melinda walking along the sidewalk. After Cynthia parked her car, she waved to her neighbor and walked up to her. Immediately she could see that Melinda had a bead of sweat that was keeping the wispy brown hairs on her forehead matted down to the skin. Melinda's jacket folded over her low hanging leather handbag, her bare arms were exposed and starting to brown in the summer sun. She was hot. Overheated.

"Did you walk home?!" Cynthia didn't mean to sound so shocked, but the idea of Melinda walking the entire distance that Cynthia had just driven seemed absurd.

Melinda smiled and waved, taking a few steps off of the sidewalk and up the Lawson's driveway. "Oh no, I took the bus, just walked from the stop at the corner."

Cynthia quickly calculated that was still a quarter mile walk. "Goodness, you must be so hot," she pulled at the silk button-down she was wearing, feeling her own skin start to prickle at the idea of walking any distance in the summer humidity.

"Oh, it isn't so bad. Thankfully it wasn't raining," Melinda smiled optimistically.

"Well, if you need a ride or something, just give me a call." Cynthia offered automatically before realizing that she probably wouldn't want to offer a ride. She hoped Melinda wouldn't take her up on it.

"Oh, thank you so much. This is just temporary," Melinda waved her hand, swatting the offer away.

"Okay. Car in the shop?" Cynthia jumped to, what seemed, the obvious conclusion.

"No, sold it actually," Melinda seemed proud to make this announcement.

"Wow, that's great," Cynthia was again saying words that didn't fit what she was thinking. Her mind was starting to tally the last time that she had seen the Ryechiks in their car. And Timothy had mentioned the van the other day, maybe it wasn't theirs after all.

"Yeah, we got a great value so I'm glad we sold it when we did, but now we're both trading off on the bus."

"Well hopefully that money can go to a better car for next time," Cynthia concluded, knowing that the two of them would need a car soon. With the summer heat only just starting to set in, the Ryechiks would become melted puddles on the sidewalk if they didn't start driving to and from work again soon. Surely, they needed a second vehicle to get around, assuming that van was Jack's. Cynthia couldn't be sure though; didn't he have a sedan too? She couldn't remember.

"Yeah, maybe," Melinda dismissed her comment. "I'm going to head in for some water," she motioned with her thumb, looking like a hitchhiker only a few yards from her own home.

"Oh of course, how rude of me," Cynthia snapped out of her train of thought. "And be sure to text me if you ever need a ride," she called after Melinda as she walked up to her own front door. Cynthia shook her head as she entered the home, cool in a palpable way, the air conditioning tingling on the bottom hairline of her neck, hitting those spots that had started to perspire in the sun. *That poor woman, forced to take the bus and walk.* Jack had better get her a car soon, it was just not right for him to not drive her home.

Timothy would never make me take the bus or walk home. She felt even more confident in her own relationship now that she had such an extreme example for comparison. Cynthia pulled out her phone and took a photo of the sleek black bottle with matte wrapping. "Fancy dinner and wine tonight?" she sent to her husband with the image attached.

She began to pull out her pots and pans. One to sauté with, one to braise in, a quart of water poured and starting to heat up. Her phone buzzed, she was alive with excitement, the extreme opposite of the desperate woman, unable to breathe under the weight of her normalcy less than 20 minutes earlier.

"Maybe tomorrow night, lots to get done." Was the response.

"Sorry : (" popped up less than a minute later.

What a roller coaster. Her marriage was better than the Ryechiks because her husband did provide for her. However, he also didn't want to spend any time with her. She felt that tightness in her throat again, another heaving gasp about to work its way out. She turned off the burners and poured the tepid water down the drain.

She fumbled with the corkscrew but eventually got the bottle open. A long swig of the red wine helped to calm her nerves. She took a decisive action; she would enjoy this bottle of wine by herself for dinner. She would have the amazing life that she wanted with her nice wines, her vacations, and her car and never let her husband make her feel normal again.

chapter **17**

TIMOTHY HAD BEEN challenged by his affection for Cynthia early in their courtship. She was always made up so beautifully and had an easy sense of humor. She dressed well, like a respectable young woman, but made her sexual prowess clear. Timothy's friends congratulated him on securing so desirable a mate.

But she wasn't always so desirable to Timothy. She would drone on about mundane drama in her circle of friends. She would drag him to the mall to go shopping, insisting on his input even when she disregarded it. Before their wedding, she spent indiscriminately even when he protested about sticking to a budget. This didn't sit right with him, but it mimicked the life of TV husbands and romantic movie male-leads. If it aped like a fairy-tale, then perhaps it really was one.

Most days the good outweighed the bad in their relationship. In the months leading up to the purchase of the house, they had been thrilled and excited to discuss the details of the purchase together. Now they were able to talk about decorating the home and additional furniture purchases to fill each room. They finally had something to say to each other, but he could tell that the material would soon run out. Timothy had to temper Cynthia's excitement by reminding her of their financial restrictions. With the mortgage, they didn't have ample cash on hand to continue to make large purchases each month. Even with the five-year payment structure of new couches and guest beds, they wouldn't be able to keep up with more monthly payments going out the door.

He wanted her to be happy and to stay happy. He wanted Cynthia to smile at him the way she used to when he would bring home flowers or buy her an unexpected gift. He needed her appreciation as much as he needed an extra $10,000 in the bank to relieve the financial pressure he was feeling. Could they make this dream house work? Could they make this *dream* work?

The timing of that rhetorical question was uncanny. As Timothy pondered a means of keeping his wife happy and ensuring he could give her the life and the lifestyle she desired, his cell phone buzzed from under a file folder on his desk.

Swiping quickly to answer before he checked the number, Timothy was greeted by an overly friendly male voice.

"Hello, this is David Quinten with First Regional Bank, is Mr. Timothy Lawson available?" This man said that he worked for the local credit union where all of the Lawson's accounts and the firm's banking accounts were held. Expecting this man's questions to relate to the legal business, Timothy was floored when the man began to explain that he was calling due to a repeated instance of his personal checking account being overdrawn. It had happened four times in the past two months and the man was tasked with calling to see if there might be a better solution that they could work on together.

At least those were the words he used, what he really meant was that the bank was monitoring his accounts because he had just barely qualified for the mortgage and now, he was short on funds. They were worried about not being able to recoup their money, and Timothy didn't blame them. He was already swimming in the deep end, so to speak, with debt before Cynthia began to insist on purchasing a home. They both had a high amount of debt to manage and adding a mortgage seemed impossible. Until his father stepped in and wrote a letter of recommendation and then agreed to co-sign the loan on the house.

The additional clout of the man who Timothy most wanted to be like, and whose approval was still so elusive, had saved the day. Of course, Timothy would never want Cynthia to find this out. He appeased the man on the phone and assured him that the problem would not persist. He had just moved and there were some extra unexpected items that needed to be purchased; surely, he would understand. The man agreed and began to go on about the credit union's program that offered free financial counseling to members to help them budget and "get back on track."

As the man continued, Timothy began to tally how much had been coming out of his checking account on a regular basis. Each of his meals out, everything they had purchased for the house, their monthly subscriptions were on the credit cards. It dawned on Timothy that his credit cards now must have larger minimum monthly payments to cause his automated bill-pay deductions to overdraw his account. He panicked and he raced to log in as the man continued to talk.

"Yes, of course," Timothy spat into the void each time the man paused to ask a question or add effect to the conversation.

His jaw dropped into his free hand as Timothy saw the full amount due on just one of his cards. As he began to realize the extent of the problem, he hurried off the phone, cutting off the man whose name he had already forgotten with an assurance that he would sign up for the free financial counseling. Over the next hour, Timothy poured through the credit card statements for his half dozen accounts. He couldn't get his mind around just how much was owed. And these were just *his* cards, *what if Cynthia was spending this much? What if she was spending next to nothing and Timothy was the sole person in the relationship leading them to financial ruin? Or, what if? What if she was spending more?*

They had kept their expenses separate for the entirety of their relationship and they hadn't changed that when they got married. He had no idea of what Cynthia was or wasn't spending, but she had been complaining that she wanted a raise. *No, she has earned a raise that is the only reason. She's not in it this bad.* Timothy's internal self-assurances were weak, but they pacified his growing anxiety for a brief moment.

Scrambling quickly to determine the size of the problem, Timothy requested credit reports for both himself and Cynthia to see how bad it was. He printed them out and put them into a file folder without looking at them carefully. He also printed out his recent credit card statements and put them into the folder as well. Before the standard workday was over, Timothy had a manila folder thick with recent printouts of his financial life. A physical representation of his consumer debt. He planned to add his latest car payment and mortgage payment paperwork to the file. Then he could get his head around this thing.

It seemed improbable that he and his wife could have that much paperwork around their regular monthly spending. Maybe something was off. Maybe someone had stolen their identity and that accounted for some of the issues. Although, if someone had been ruining their credit, they would never have been approved for the home loan. Then again, they didn't qualify on their own.

Timothy struggled with the need to know just how bad it was, and his desire to push it aside and hope that it would resolve itself. He had spent four hours, time that he could have been working on his current caseload and billing to clients, on a personal matter. He could ill-afford a paycheck reflecting less than 160 hours in two weeks. He would need to come in over the weekend to make up some time.

The devil on his shoulder made a different suggestion. Timothy added those hours under the code for his current case with Hydroline. He would still come in over the weekend to get the work done, but he intended to bill that time as well. The big corporation could afford to pay him a little extra, after all, he needed the money. How else was he going to make his accounts balance?

Timothy headed home early that day at 6:30 pm, surprising and delighting his wife who arrived home after him for a change. As Timothy rounded the turn into the neighborhood, he noticed a large blue SUV leaving with dark tint on the windows. He couldn't recognize the vehicle as one of the neighbors, but he was still getting to know the area. What made this SUV stick out in his mind was that he could have sworn he had seen it before. As it passed him, he spotted a realtor's magnet on the side door. The face and the name were vaguely familiar: Ryan Moore. Why did that name ring a bell? Why did it make him so nervous?

chapter **18**

THEIR WEEKEND STARTED with an ambitious to-do list and a trip to the local home improvement store for supplies. The downstairs was still that bright mustard yellow and Cynthia wanted to select paint samples so that she could narrow down the color choices for the painters. She was also hoping to find some storage systems for the mudroom and top of the line energy efficient appliances for the laundry. Timothy tagged along to offer… support? Guidance? He didn't know the first thing about home improvement, but he was eager to please his wife and provide his… credit card. That's it, that's what he was doing there, financing her whims.

The Lawsons browsed each aisle carefully, letting the strong aroma of fresh lumber and paint thinner fill their nostrils, providing them with a brief high. Timothy wanted to be more of a handy-man, a man's man. He wanted to be able to explain something to Cynthia about a project that would be helpful to the two of them, some knowledge that he could be confident in sharing. But he didn't know any of these things. If only his father could have shown him, but the elder Lawson had been busy building a legal empire. Everything in their household had been outsourced: a contractor for major repairs, a cook for meals, a maid for tidying, a lawn service for the estate. What Timothy had learned was to hire someone, which could have been a beneficial skill to learn if he too was starting his own business and had sufficient funds with which to employ said workers. But none of that applied to him.

Timothy silently glanced at all of the various tools and solvents as Cynthia ushered him through several aisles. Once they arrived at the paint section, he let her take the lead on which colors she thought would go best in the home. He trusted her style, she always looked so well done and put together. A small wave of pride rushed over him and he set his self-pity aside to offer helpful little comments as Cynthia held up several paint chips.

They had agreed to tackle the most pressing things first; on the top of their list was painting the downstairs. The bright color strained their eyes. It had to go. Cynthia wanted to linger and look at ornate dining room tables. She convinced Timothy to stop by a salvage yard to see if they could find some reclaimed wood to use for a custom dining table that would have more character. She had seen such treasure hunts on television, but her search did not pan out. Cynthia made a note on the list that they would need to find an interior designer who could find such a piece for them. If it couldn't be found, they could always buy new and then distress the wood.

Inherently, what she was saying didn't add up to Timothy. You bought stuff to make new wood look old, and that gave it character? It seemed off to him, but Timothy decided not to press any further. He was content to finish the first project early and get on with a mindless afternoon of TV watching.

After purchasing the pint-sized samples of paint and the narrow paint brushes that would fit into the little cans, the Lawsons returned to their new home. Cynthia was giddy with excitement. Their first big project in the new house. She stroked the synthetic fibers of the new paint brushes against the palm of her hand the entire way home. She enjoyed the smooth and silky feeling of the virgin brush, tickling her skin. She enjoyed the shine of the faux brass that held the bristles to the wooden handle. She loved that Timothy's car was starting to smell like paint, an aroma that she associated with hard work.

Once they arrived home, Cynthia busied herself by finding newspapers to put on the ground in several key spots in the house. She wanted to do test swatches in several rooms to see how the paint would look in different lights. Timothy was amused by her excitement. Cynthia hadn't been this eager to start a project since they had planned their wedding. She seemed to thrive when she had a project to tackle, something to design. He made a mental note to compliment her on her project management skills later. He forgot to do this, so Cynthia never heard these words of admiration.

After each room was set up with a healthy array of newspapers acting as drop cloths, the Lawsons went to each of the designated corners to paint a three-square inch swatch of each of the sample paint colors. There was a muted taupe, a pale blue pebble, and a margarine-tinted cream. Each color was neutral, Cynthia continued to reiterate the same few lines that she had read online about how neutral colors will allow their minds to be calmer and more at rest. Timothy already felt calm, he felt so calm that he could have walked out their front door, down the driveway, out of the neighborhood, and kept walking until his feet blistered and his legs gave out. He felt so calm that he could just leave and never come back.

Maybe he didn't recognize that calmness was actually a feeling of detachment, a process his inner-psyche had started ever since he received that call from the bank.

Cynthia insisted that they should let the paint dry and revisit the color selections in a few days after they had time to get used to the color being on the walls. Timothy found the harsh difference between the mustard yellow and the cool pale tones to be too much for his eyes to handle, the rods and cones in his retina were misfiring, leaving his vision splotchy as though he had just seen the flash of a camera.

Outside they could hear the usual domestic sounds of suburbia: a skateboard rolling and clacking down the smooth and then abruptly un-level sidewalk blocks; a dog barking as it was being taken for a walk by its owner; the faint but gradually increasing volume of a lawnmower. As Cynthia headed upstairs with one of the remaining boxes, Timothy stepped into the garage and opened the door. The white daylight blanched and his eyes were scarred once again.

Timothy tinkered and organized. He had received several large power tools as wedding gifts: power drill, circular saw, and a power sander. Equipped to be able to tackle any project his wife could think of, proba-bly. As he tried to find the best way to display his tools so that they were easy to find and access, he continued to hear the rhythmic droning of a lawnmower somewhere nearby. It grew closer; louder and louder until it sounded like it was about to run him over. Just when he thought that the sound couldn't possibly get any louder, just when he was about to turn around to see where it was, it began to grow quieter again. This process repeated for the better part of an hour. The sound made him feel calm. After days of being trapped inside a silent office, he was grateful for the normalcy of noise.

The engine to the lawnmower cut, voices of children playing down the street drifted through the neighborhood again. Timothy stood back and saw that he liked what he had started with the pegboard and wanted to end his task there. Someone in the neighborhood had just finished their chores, his brain reacted and told him to stop as well.

Timothy ventured down the driveway to check the mail. He looked around to see if any neighbors were out that he could wave to or introduce himself to. He wanted to make this house a true home, he wanted to be a respected member of a community, he wanted the things he was supposed to want. It looked like Dan and his family were away that weekend. Timothy turned to his right; he saw Jack emerging from his backyard.

"Howdy!" Timothy waved.

"Hey man," Jack walked over and began the normal niceties with Timothy. How was his weekend going? Getting settled in all right? Timothy mentioned his work organizing tools at which Jack's face lit up like a small child's. The men walked into the garage to wonder at the spectacle of toys that Timothy had arranged. The two bonded over the power tools as so many men do. Jack nodded in approval at the arrangement on the pegboard. This modern ritual of male interaction was perfectly delightful for both.

"You're lucky man. I miss my power tools." Jack shook his head in a cartoonish manner, as though he had seen the expression practiced so many times on television that it had now been incorporated into his lexicon of non-verbal communication.

"Miss them, what happened?"

"I loaned my best power drill to my neighbor-"

"The Mahaskals?"

"Yes," Jack gestured to the garage around them, acknowledging the past ownership of the domicile. "I loaned it out, months passed, I didn't get it back." As Jack moved his hand, his blistered and bloodied knuckles were visible beneath a white bandage covering his palm.

"That's not cool," Timothy was eager to agree as he imagined his own frustration in that situation of non-returned tools.

"Well, no. It wasn't cool. But I also realized that in all that time I never needed to use that item. So eventually I stopped keeping track. I sold off most of my larger tools. I still have the lawn equipment, since I use that fairly often in the summers."

"Oh," Timothy didn't know what to say. He would have assumed that Jack still held a grudge about the non-returned items. But it didn't seem to bother him. Timothy couldn't relate to that notion; he would have been knocking on the door (his own now) every day until his expensive tools were returned. He nodded in feigned agreement.

"What happened to your hand?" was the next thought in Timothy's head and it popped out of his mouth before he could stop himself.

"Oh, just a little trouble in the garage the other day," Jack tucked his arm behind his back. Before Timothy could inquire further, Jack quickly excused himself to go and finish putting his lawn equipment away.

Timothy took this as his cue to mow his own lawn. "Ah, speaking of which, I had better get out there!" It was already well past noon, which meant it would only get hotter and hotter until the sun finally surrendered beneath the horizon.

"Yeah, good luck," Jack walked out and moved his arm so that it was out of sight.

"Cool man. And if you ever need to borrow anything just let me know, alright?" Timothy waved as Jack passed from sight.

Mission of the afternoon: partially accomplished. Tools starting to get organized. Made friends with the neighbor. Their one-on-one interaction was much better than the forced coupling at dinner the other week.

Perhaps that was because Cynthia and Melinda were so different. Even in his mind, Timothy knew he didn't mean in a good way, sometimes he wondered why Cynthia was so intent on her looks. There was taking pride in your appearance and then there was looking for attention. He never knew what side of that line she was really on. He pondered this recurring worry as he poured the gas into the mower, pumped it through the engine, and yanked at the cord. He mowed the right side of the lawn that he shared with Dan and worked through the backyard; the sound of Bentley yapping from inside the closed doors penetrated the roar of the engine every few beats.

As Timothy worked methodically over to the left side yard, he realized that it was already cropped. It appeared that Jack had gone out of his way to mow the full side yard, not just his share. Timothy cut the engine and smiled. *That guy is alright.*

Over dinner, they discussed the progress on the house. Cynthia was planning to head over to a discount home goods store the next day to see if she could find some decorations for the guest bedroom and bathroom. They had so many more rooms to furnish now. She wondered how it would ever be ready for guests to see.

"We don't need it to be perfect honey. Our friends will know that it is a work in progress." This comment only partially pacified Cynthia. Timothy changed the subject to his efforts in the garage. He found it odd how proud he was of this mundane task. Perhaps that pride came from the same place within him that stored his insecurities. He was worried that he would fail at a task that so many other men would find second-nature. Having his own approval, and the outside approval of Jack made him feel validated. It was a feeling that he experienced so infrequently that his body seemed to glow when he felt that warm reassurance pass over him.

Cynthia was notably concerned about his conversation with Jack. Given her suspicions about the demise of the Mahaskals she didn't want this potentially dangerous man to be spending time with her husband.

"Great, now he is going to want to borrow your tools all the time."

"Oh no. I mean I offered him the chance, but he said he had sold off all of his tools because he didn't need them."

"Oh," Cynthia tried to cover up her assumption with antipathy. She didn't like being wrong. Even though this was something that her husband should have understood, she never opened up to him about it. To Cynthia, intimacy was only about physical pleasure. She hadn't experienced any positive relationship where she could share her innermost worries and fears, her self-criticisms, her pride. And because of that, Timothy never experienced that either. Nothing about their conversations was intimate; there were no glances to steal or unspoken burning in their eyes. Cynthia pushed the food around her plate to avoid acknowledging her unintended and completely unimportant false assumption.

"But he did say that his old neighbor, the one who used to live here, had borrowed one of his tools and took forever to return it. So, I bet if he did ask, he would be really sensitive to that."

"Hmm," Cynthia's imagination had been piqued. "I wonder if that is why he doesn't know where they are now so that we can forward their mail."

"Honestly, we should just throw it out. It's mostly magazines anyway." Timothy was irritated by Cynthia's obsession over the forwarding mail. It was like a gnat that wouldn't fly away no matter how many times you swatted your hand, this inane conversation would never die.

"It's a federal offense." Her terse words had become a regular addition to their conversations. Where they had once been sweet and kind to each other, it was clear that Cynthia's patience for Timothy had a lifetime limit and she was doling out the remaining amount judiciously.

"It's only a federal offense to open mail that isn't addressed to you. We don't have a forwarding address. We should either pitch it or do a 'return to sender'."

Timothy finished the food on his plate and wiped his mouth with the paper napkin. The enjoyment he had from a few moments ago, had dissipated. It was like his efforts to work-out; of course, she wouldn't care about his small achievements around the house. It was stupid to be so proud of such a small thing, but for a man who never had to use his hands, setting up that garage was his big accomplishment. He looked over at the closed door that led from the kitchen into the garage. That was his domain, his happy place. Cynthia didn't understand that he wanted to explain it to her, but he realized she would just as soon laugh at him instead of patting him on the back.

"OK, but it's still weird that Dan said they were great friends and now the Ryechiks don't even know where they live. That's kind of strange."

"Well, our old neighbors don't know our new address." Timothy was done with the conversation. He excused himself from the table and started to clean his plate.

Unable to accept that her opinion would go unheard, Cynthia pursued him across the open room. "Yeah, but no one would ever think to say that we were close with them. We weren't."

"Okay."

Timothy hardly ever raised his voice, so when he did it was a signal to back down. His voice hadn't necessarily been loud, but it was finite, his agitation was evident in the monosyllabic response.

That evening they went to sleep, exhausted from their physical labor and their conversational dysfunctions. Cynthia was genuinely happy to have had Timothy's attention for an entire morning. Not to suggest that she was attention hungry, she certainly was, but she also began to miss his company when he spent so much time at work. Of course, she had pushed him too much. She had annoyed him at dinner. *How had she forgotten how to have a conversation with him? Was that it? When had that knowledge been extracted from her brain?* It must have been after the honeymoon. The symbolic honeymoon was clearly over now, but when had that newly-wed bliss worn off?

They fell asleep quickly but Cynthia woke with a start after a few hours. She felt something, small and almost imperceptible, but she felt it. A tiny flicking sound registered in her ear and she jolted up immediately. Certain that the two-inch oblong dark object on her pillow was an insect, the most loathsome insect, she yelled. Quickly she began to swat at her ear, afraid that perhaps another one had crawled into the recesses. *Wretched roach.* She kicked her legs as she began to feel every stitch of the sheets on her skin, worried that they were all insects instead.

"What is it?" Timothy muttered groggily.

"There's one on my pillow!" Cynthia strained her voice in a breathy panic.

"No there isn't. Go back to sleep," he barely lifted his arm as though he was reaching to comfort her, but the sleep had weighted his limb and he missed her completely.

"I know that has happened before, but I swear there is one on my pillow right now!" Cynthia was pleading with him to help. This had in fact happened before, she would be half asleep and see a bug on her leg, on her arm, on the edge of the bed, on her pillow. Each time she would shriek in terror and beg Timothy to help her. Each time he would turn on the light and it would be gone.

Timothy groaned this time and rolled over to turn on his bedside lamp.

The bulb cast a soft yellow glow over their pillows, both of them now sitting up in bed. The dark and rumpled crease in Cynthia's pillow had replaced the insect.

"It was right there, I swear." She wanted to show him that she was right; she wasn't some crazy lady freaking out for nothing in the middle of the night. She desperately wanted – needed – him to believe her.

"Uh huh," Timothy turned off the light and slept on his side, facing away from her. Left with her fears and her thoughts, Cynthia stared at the ceiling and covered her ears with her hands, trying desperately to forget this latest mini-trauma, all the while not being able to think of anything else. Timothy fell back to sleep quickly, dreaming of a life without Cynthia that included restful nights, a flush bank account, and the ability to find a woman who would complement him.

chapter 19

SUMMER AFTERNOONS, THE highlight of the year for schoolchildren when they are free from the daily routine of school, the nostalgic playtime for adults who still anticipate the season with glee, an aberrant effect after years of being conditioned to count down until summer arrived. Jack and Melinda had yet to outgrow the anticipatory giddiness that they associated with summer. They were far more productive before noon than most other people, especially on weekends. Their weekends were the domain for their life's work. In the preceding months, they had both grown more brazen in their personal views. They started to apologize less; they weren't exactly sure what they had ever been apologizing for. Their thoughts were just that, thoughts. Their opinions were theirs; they certainly didn't owe anyone an explanation. Their plan was theirs as well, they were solely responsible for it.

This state of calm and acceptance wasn't always present in their lives, and even that summer it was tenuous. It felt like everything they had worked for could all just slip away, could be snatched from them in an instant. They felt a manic pressure to sprint to the finish line, as it were. Years earlier, they had both been less sure of their plan. Melinda often retreated into herself and felt the adolescent sting of, once again, not having many girlfriends to confide in. An immature worry, but it was one that she carried with her for years. Jack on the other hand would get frustrated. His boss would comment on his attire and suggest an updated wardrobe. These slight jabs only incited Jack to action, instead of pressuring him to venture further into the vortex that trapped so many, he fought against it. Resisting the centrifugal force of the consumerism and retail-focused world around him.

"I'm tired of having to defend myself, to defend our lifestyle to others. Why? Because I am awake, because I am conscious about the choices I make instead of following the herd, blindly consuming and spending? No, I'm tired of it!" Jack had reached his limit one day. Passed over for a promotion because he didn't look the part. He was irate, explosively mad at the system for mandating a minimum spend of one thousand dollars a quarter on the latest in men's fashion. He was apoplectic, ranting to Melinda about how he would only want the promotion for the raise and that he didn't care about their status symbols. Only he did, he worked hard, why shouldn't he be awarded the trappings of the modern American workplace? It was a complex frustration, he felt duped by the system as though he was now supposed to wallow in self-pity and then pull himself up and work that much harder for the carrot being dangled before him.

"It isn't about being the hardest worker, or the smartest person in the room. It's about playing their game. If you want to win that game, then the rules are pretty clear. If you don't care about the game at all, then you can disregard the rules, but you can't expect the get ahead. Or-" Melinda paused in her explanation for effect, "you can work their system to your benefit and leave the playing board whenever you like."

The plan was a seed nestled in the fertile soil of their minds at the time, cut off from the resources that would one-day feed and nourish that idea until it blossomed, until it could burst forth and become reality.

That had been several years earlier when they had that fateful discussion, only a week after that Jack had stumbled upon a blog. This then led to a rabbit's hole of other information and websites. Over the following years, the Ryechiks had fine-tuned their dream and then, suddenly, it was a reality just off in the horizon. It was the big red boat coming into the harbor with the sun rising just behind it. That summer each moment felt surreal; would this be the last batch of oranges that they would pick from the local grove that they loved to frequent? Would this be the final few weeks to run up the hill that they both dreaded on their workouts?

Savoring each moment of the day, the Ryechiks moved about the space that contained them in a visible stupor, as they had when they were first in love, smitten with the idea of each other. Thankfully, most of their possessions had been given away so they had far fewer things to trip over, although that summer was not without incident. Melinda was daydreaming of THE BIG DAY and walked into the kitchen island, leaving a blue then yellow bruise just above her elbow.

She was aimlessly puttering into the kitchen to start preparing for the barbecue they planned to have that evening. A hot summer Saturday night with hot dogs and hamburgers. Melinda was excited, she was hoping that they would have been able to test out the camping grill that she and Jack would soon use on the road, but they had to return it to the store for a quick repair. She chopped the lettuce and tomato for the burgers before moving onto dicing the onions for the hotdogs. Moving methodically, as always, Melinda reminded herself to stay grounded so that she didn't venture off into her day-dream and slice off the tip of her finger.

The various parts of the meal, still to be assembled, were ready to be carried out to the grill by 7:00 pm. This was Melinda's favorite time of day during the summer because the sun would dazzle off the pond. She left the mildly cool interior of the house, nearly impossible to fully air-condition in the summer, for the dry and breezy heat of the evening. The air was parched, or maybe that was what Melinda thought because she was thirsty. Isn't it funny how humans so often project their own feelings onto the inanimate and intangible elements around them?

The Lawsons were also taking advantage of the summer bliss by the pond. Cynthia was lounging in a reclining deck chair with an e-reader in her lap and her tiny dog at her feet. Melinda was surprised to see her in such a relaxed position, and with her hair twisted up in a bun. She made a smart comment in her mind, then chided herself for even thinking such a rude thought.

When Jack fired up the grill, he waved to Timothy who signaled back, tongs in hand.

"Meat!" Jack gruffed and pounded his chest once. Timothy mimed him and the two seemed to enjoy their caveman impersonations. The men-folk were happy. The women-folk were stand-offish. As the flames finished their work on the food that both couples were preparing, they gravitated to the picnic bench that sat between the two houses near the edge of the pond. They ate a meal together, the men mostly discussing their methods for seasoning the meat. Breaking the silence, Cynthia offered Melinda a glass of wine.

Melinda demurred politely, but Cynthia just had to know.

"No wine, huh? Any particular reason?" her voice was thick with insinuation and, unknown to her, insult.

Melinda was barren. She and Jack tried to conceive years earlier. They first tried the natural method and when that didn't work they took to explicit tantra instructions regarding ejaculatory efficiency, modulated their diet to ensure that they had the best baby-making hormones and enzymes, and when all else failed, they finally prayed. But no baby ever materialized in Melinda's pink and otherwise healthy womb. They only shared their struggle with a few select friends, most of whom were extremely sympathetic, until they had their own children and just got too caught up in the day-to-day of parenting.

As if their inefficacy wasn't enough, they also had an overwhelming mass of content constantly shoved at them. First, it was the advertisements targeted at young married couples "just like them" who were expected to be expecting by their age. Then it was the constant news stories on baby names and gene-splicing, and the commercials, and the reality TV shows. Melinda often found articles in the most unexpected of magazines with women highlighting their struggle to conceive. Of course, those women in the magazines turned to in-vitro because maintaining a healthy weight, eating right, exercising, and *gasp* adoption were completely out of the question.

Melinda called herself pathetic, the amount of time that they had spent talking about something that wasn't a given. She and Jack had planned for this one-day child as though their existence was guaranteed. When this child never materialized, she felt robbed, but how could she be robbed of something that never existed?

She couldn't stand it, she stopped reading about it, she stopped talking about it, and, fortunately, she had a husband who let her. They found something new to create together, and it was sitting, heavy and ready for action, in their garage, only feet away from where they sat eating their grilled food with the Lawsons.

Melinda had a practiced response to Cynthia's question and gave a vehement, "Oh no," as if to suggest that she wouldn't want children. That couldn't have been further from the truth, but she certainly wasn't going to let Cynthia know that.

Having artfully deflected Cynthia's inquiry, Melinda asked her how 'things were going at work.' A question with no depth or personality, but one that prompted a torrent of words from Cynthia. Speaking between scoops of the sweet and soggy baked beans, barely leaving any room for oxygen, she explained her delayed promotion and raise.

Exasperated by her own repeated litany of reasons why she deserved a raise, Cynthia finally blurted out her backup solution. Pregnancy. If she could just get pregnant now, she could quit working in a few months.

Leaning in to confide in Melinda within earshot of the men who were comparing the varied amber hues in their beers, Cynthia told her the real reason why that plan was on hold.

"Timothy says I need to work a little longer before we can afford to have kids." Melinda nodded and passed a half smile at this comment. She shrugged her shoulders with sympathy, maybe Cynthia would think she was in the same boat. Hadn't their mother's generation tried to open the door to women doing exactly what they wanted: be a mother if you want to be a mother, be a working mother if you want to be a working mother. But, the idea of having a child as a means of avoiding work made Melinda's skin crawl.

"But you can never save enough money for kids, right?"

Melinda began to feel like a bobble-head doll, her chin moving up and down in an easy cadence. Opposite her was Cynthia, optimistic and misunderstood, feeling as though she could finally connect with another woman. She always had a trouble keeping girlfriends and couldn't figure out why.

Trying to not be rude and hog the conversation, Cynthia needled further. "So, when are you and Jack going to have little ones?"

Melinda took a bite of food, chewing slowly, holding up her index finger to signal for a moment's pause in the conversation. "Well, if the time is right, then it will just happen then."

That told Cynthia enough, they can't have kids and they are upset about it. Finally, she got the message loud and clear, back off.

Cynthia sighed and changed the conversation to Melinda's work. In that moment, as she tried to remember what Melinda did for a living, she almost envied her neighbor. Cynthia viewed having children as a prison sentence. If you want to stop working, you have to have babies and then you have to put up with taking care of them. You do get to have wonderful gift showers and time off of work and lots of fun parties to plan, but she didn't feel genuinely excited about the prospect of getting big (ger) and cleaning up someone else's poop. She didn't get excited about the potential for sleepless nights, especially with Timothy's schedule, he would never help her. It didn't warm her heart to think of being a mom, but she liked the idea of staying at home. *If only that were socially acceptable.*

If she didn't have a great first impression of Cynthia before, she downright couldn't stand her now. Melinda wanted so much to tell Cynthia that life was about so much more than money and clothes and using kids to have parties. *That* woman as a mother, Melinda cringed at the thought.

Melinda's mother was memorialized in the Ryechik household in two items: an antique lamp that had been in the family since before World War I and an embroidered wall hanging that read: "Early to bed and early to rise will make you healthy, wealthy, and wise." Widowed at a young age with Melinda to look after, her mother had built an emotional wall and never allowed herself to love again.

Until she discovered online shopping. Then she fell in love and fell hard. The regular deliveries made her feel fancy. And when she died at the young age of sixty-two, she left behind a mountain of debt that was poised to bury Melinda until a long-forgotten insurance policy was redeemed. Melinda loved her mother, but now avoided reminiscing or thinking of her at all because of the recency of the betrayal her massive debt left in its wake.

She also avoided the topic because of the things she never wanted to risk saying to Jack. Both being thrifty, the two had spent the early years of their marriage worried over her mother's finances. When would they have to bear the burden of her spending habit, would she just move in one day and become a wedge between them? With her mother's untimely death, Melinda was crushed. Not only for her loss, but also for the relief she felt. Jack was quick to console her and was patient in her slow grieving process. Melinda's initial reflex was to push him away, call him out for being so critical of her mother, and accuse him of harboring a joy at her mother's death.

You must be so glad now that she won't be able to move in with us and risk spending any of your precious stockpile. She bit her tongue. Such vitriol would have been fueled by grief and would have forced that wedge between them anyway. So, Melinda mourned, fought through the fog of emptiness to stay happy. *Fake it until you make it,* was her motto. Until one day, she was just happy again. And with their Big Project to work on together, in frustrated moments she thought of it as Jack's project, but it was something they shared, and she was able to focus her energies on something worthwhile again.

Enough money to have kids? Melinda chuckled at Cynthia's comment in her mind. *Honey, if you knew what we had saved up for you wouldn't ever question what is possible again.*

PART 3

Envy

Months later, after the inquiry had been resolved, a young couple entered a convenience store in South Tampa. Both wearing sunglasses and baseball caps, the clerk immediately noted their resemblance to the Lawsons. He had seen them all over the local news for months, pretty much anyone in the area could have identified their photos, but he was so certain that they were the Lawsons. He pulled the grainy security camera footage and sent it around to his friends, and the local news station. A story that had made a small blip on the national radar was reignited.

Oh, poor choice of words.

The story was news again and more Lawson sightings were reported over the following months. They became the new big-foot, everyone was so sure that they saw them. This led to an excavation of the blast site to find the bodies and prove to the world, and their creditors, that they were in fact deceased. There was no way of bringing the bodies back up for DNA testing, but there were two decaying corpses in the pit. Photos were provided to the police and the banks and insurance companies that made specific inquiries; they were prohibited from being released to the news media. It was hard to see who they had been, but there were definitely two bodies down there. Logically, these had to be the Lawsons. Right?

chapter **20**

J ACK PULLED INTO the driveway after a long day at work. Seemingly
elongated by his exponentially growing exasperation as *the day* approached. With each hour that his life ticked away at his desk, he couldn't
help but feel the nature of his imposter's rouse; his polite camouflage
dripping off of him like a synthetic disguise, revealing his true self. With
each status report, each paper pushed, each meeting to brainstorm new
ways to do the same thing, he felt that he was selling off another piece of
his soul. What was planned, what was ahead, was the only way that he
could see to buy it back.

Sitting in the van, the last bits of the engine whimpering into silence,
he thought about what he and Melinda were planning to do. Was it reck-
less, were they the ones in the wrong? For so long they had felt as though
it was a good thing that they were different from everyone else that they
knew. He thought that they were awake, aware of all that was being pushed
on them and the illusion of the American Dream that they were being sold.
But, maybe there was a reason that everyone else was running to catch that
dream. What if he and Melinda were wrong and what they were planning
to do would ruin their lives?

When had the planning actually begun? He couldn't recall clearly, it
was an idea that had been in the deep recesses of his mind for so long, that
one day it just seemed like the thing that he had wanted to do for as long
as he could remember.

Maybe it was after Melinda's first miscarriage. Maybe it was after his
company so carelessly laid off employees the week after the former CEOs
lavish $100k retirement party. They themselves couldn't pinpoint the
moment when they changed so fundamentally. They had the date of the

first post on their website as some kind of marker, but that was after years of work. Jack had started to tinker with the idea, but it was Melinda who hit the "publish" button on that first post.

Like any person in the 21st century with an idea and a passion, they had a blog. They kept this secret from their families though, knowing that they wouldn't understand. They cultivated a small following within their little blog bubble and enjoyed the camaraderie that was so lacking in their day-to-day lives.

On the outside, the Ryechiks appeared to have the same wants and desires as the rest of their generation. But on the inside, within their house that also sat on Hurley Pond, they were apart. They weren't willing to abide the prevailing American way of life. They were separate from the crowd. Their thoughts had begun to splinter from the herd. The confluence of impacts on their life had forged them into what they were becoming. Their metamorphosis would be final upon completion of their task.

Even over the weekend, Melinda had wavered for a moment, shouldn't she try to look more like Cynthia and be the wife that society expected her to be? Should she wear make-up more often and style her hair every day for him? The insecurities that they both had about not quite fitting in ran deep, and only the other could truly understand what their partner was going through.

Jack reassured Melinda and had considered stopping to get her some flowers or some other conventional gift on the way home. But, with their big day approaching, he knew funds would be limited. Instead, he printed out a recipe at work for her favorite dessert, he knew they had all of the ingredients.

Finally, after several moments of introspection, and debating with himself if baking Melinda a treat would be a sufficient gesture, he decided to stop second-guessing the plan. This is what they believed in, and they were both committed to seeing it through, no matter what obstacles were thrown their way. He accepted that he would have doubts again, but he knew that what he was doing was right.

After putting all of the ingredients together and popping them into the oven, hoping that the aroma would greet his wife once she arrived home from work, Jack headed out to the garage to tinker a bit more.

Weeks of cutting and molding, soldering and hammering, were paying off and now only the final touches needed to be applied before a thorough test-run ahead of their big day. Jack crossed off items on the chalkboard that hung on the garage wall as each task was completed. A man and his plan, or at least the physical manifestation of the vehicle that would deliver them to their event horizon. He stood under the bald light of the garage, his muscles taut, his hands gritty from the few mechanisms that he fiddled with; he counted the remaining items to cross off.

Only a few more remained, they were getting closer. The last item on the board read, "confirm all day-of tasks on paper, erase board." He confirmed that the paper list that was taped to the particle board shelf at his eye level started with, "drop board off at local library with chalk."

Yes, the day when they would execute their plan was close, and even though it hadn't originally been part of the plan, the day when the Lawsons would perish was also getting closer.

chapter **21**

IT TURNED OUT to be a rough week for the ill-fated Lawsons. Cynthia had requested a meeting with her boss to discuss her quarterly plans. Her actual intent had been to request a raise, so she had spent the time that should have been dedicated to preparing those plans, in rehearsal. She practiced in the bathroom mirror what she would say and then how she would expect her boss to react. These practiced conversations ranged from effortless to confrontational. Cynthia planned for each possible response to the request and ultimately refined her ask to a raise and a title change, accepting that the amount of money she was asking for would likely be reserved for someone with a higher-ranking position in the company.

When the time came for the meeting, Cynthia softly tapped on the door and asked if her boss was ready. The fair-skinned and frizzy-haired boss waved Cynthia in and directed her to take a seat. After asking for the reports, Cynthia quickly dove into her rehearsed statements. Her boss abruptly cut her off.

"I thought this was a meeting about your quarterly plans, do you have them available?" Her boss was a tired-looking woman of medium height, medium weight, and medium personality. If she was less personable, Cynthia may have been better able to communicate with her, using quick questions and providing quick answers. However, because this woman was neither friendly nor standoffish, Cynthia never knew where she stood in her esteem.

"Yes, my plans are almost complete, but with each new quarter we get further into the year without discussing what goals you want to me to accomplish or what I need to do to demonstrate that I am ready to take my career to the next level." Cynthia offered a nervous smile; maybe if she didn't project too much confidence her boss would understand how difficult it was for her to even broach the subject.

"I really don't have time to have this conversation." Shut down. This was not a scenario that Cynthia had rehearsed.

"Oh okay," she stood quickly and tried to exit the office to hide her embarrassment and frustration.

"Cynthia," she heard her boss call her to turn back around. Maybe she would empathize with her and recall a time earlier in her own career when she was in need of guidance or mentorship. Maybe she would suggest a better time to meet on the subject. "Can you make sure to send me those plans by the end of the day?"

"Yes," Cynthia stammered as she nodded, practically bowing, on her way out.

"And please close my door behind you," her boss's head was already buried back into the paperwork on her desk.

Humiliated, Cynthia returned to her desk and slouched down into her chair, carefully avoiding eye contact with her coworkers. *I can't believe she doesn't see the value I bring to the team.*

Her initial frustration was turning into rage. Cynthia racked her brain for what more she could do, the idea of finishing her plans and submitting them before the end of the day did not make the list.

Taking a cursory glance at the people that occupied the cubicles around her, Cynthia knew she was better than her coworkers. *I dress for the job I want. Clearly, I am sending the correct signals.* This was Cynthia's reality.

The perception that her teammates had of her would come out as soon as the allegations started flying. She would often wear tight skirts and low-cut tops, which isn't a crime or even a reason to dislike a person, nevertheless, her coworkers did dislike her for it. Her flirtations with Erik were obvious and when interviewed by the police, people were quick to point out a rumored affair. Even though it was false, in action, the damage had been done. Cynthia Lawson was disgraced from beyond her grave. If only one of them would have pulled her aside while she was alive to give her the guidance she so clearly needed, she might not have been home at the time of the explosion.

But this was the path that Cynthia was on. She spent the afternoon searching for other jobs online. She entered a minimum salary amount into the requirements and began scrolling. Her other requirements were not listed on the standard search fields. She wanted to work for a glamorous company or an exciting product. She wanted to attend a fancy holiday party each year and receive a stipend for her cell phone. She wanted a job that was worthy of her time. Hours passed and she had saved a few to look into over the weekend. Cynthia thought about texting Timothy to tell him that her meeting earlier had been a bust, but didn't want to admit her defeat. It was good that she didn't, because Timothy was already spiraling into a blind panic.

Stress weighed on Timothy as though all of the files on his desk were actually strapped to his back. The case against Hydroline was impressive. He would need to use all of the legal maneuverings in his arsenal to win. His father and uncle would be excellent resources. They had fought against big companies in their hay-day; they would be able to give him the needed perspective on how to prepare to litigate for their client. He didn't want to seem weak, he wanted to wait until he had a better handle on things before bringing them in.

It turns out that Hydroline was most likely culpable for the problems that the citizens in the class-action lawsuit levied against the company. It was odd for the Lawson firm to be defending a corporation, but this was the reality that they found themselves in. Having built a reputation for battling big companies that spoiled the environment, Hydroline had sought out the help of Lawson & Lawson so that their P.R. team could spin the environmental legacy of the firm into a headline. *Environmental Law group defends Hydroline.* Who better to tell a judge that they are innocent? Timothy shook his head at the idea. The jargon was all muddled. Then again, the press usually didn't pick up on those subtleties.

It seemed that increased mineral extractions by Hydroline have given way to increased sinkhole activity across the state. This had left homes uninhabitable, neighborhoods under a flood of foreclosures, and in one very serious incident a man swallowed by his own house, never to be seen again, lost to the abyss. Timothy had a map of the state in his office with red marks for each of the sinkholes that the citizens were alleging that Hydroline caused. It looked like the state had a rash across a wide band of land. There were also blue marks for each of the mining sites. There was a correlation, but as Timothy planned to argue, correlation and causation are two very different things.

Timothy had been working longer and longer hours, leaving Cynthia at home to watch her shows (all on basic cable even though they had the most premium package). As a result, he was also spending more time in the sports bar across the street for dinner. More expensive meals and generous tips, more time with Kellyanne, and a subtle addition to his waistline.

After his eyes refused to read another line about soil composition and earth cover collapse, he turned his attention to his own personal finances. It was an equally odious task, but one that was troubling him. Even as he handed over his credit card for his take-out dinner that evening, he felt an anxiety, *what if the card is declined? What was he doing to his own budget?* He gorged himself on fried food and now had a paunch to show for it. *Wasn't he doing the same to his bank account?* Self-destruction doesn't always have to be in the form of alcoholism or drugs, no the Lawsons were building their own guillotine without any chemical intervention.

As he began to pull together a spreadsheet of their regular expenses, all billed on company time, Timothy began to wonder how he could explain it all to Cynthia. He munched on a cold french-fry as he considered every other option. Without her bringing in more money immediately, they would have to cut back on their spending. He printed out the plan and texted his wife that he was on his way home. A late start to their Friday evening together and he knew it would not be a relaxing night at all.

He rehearsed his words carefully as he drove home on the emptied-out highways, abandoned by a swarm of commuters hours earlier. With only the empty stares of the billboard models to practice to, Timothy failed to build the confidence he would need to face Cynthia and her expectations. *We need to sell one of the cars and carpool to work, heck our offices are across the street from one another.*

Although that plan falls apart if she got a new job, he corrected himself.

We need to cut our monthly subscriptions. Her endless gym memberships, yoga passes, and spin class payments that were all going unused had to go. *We need to bring our lunch and eat dinner at home. It won't happen overnight, but it could right the ship.* And then, once things got better, they could go back to their daily lunches out.

When he pulled into the drive, he felt secure that he had the perfectly crafted speech to give her. He had the numbers printed out to reference. This would work.

His plans fell apart only a few moments into his speech. Cynthia focused on the television, only managing to wave as he entered the house through the garage.

"Sorry I'm late," he managed as he put the papers on the counter with one hand, petting a frantic and excited Bentley with the other.

"Pizza is in the fridge," her voice announced to him, she wasn't visible behind the plush couch.

"Ok, I'll grab some in a minute."

"Uh huh," she was clearly entranced in the movie that she was watching, it looked like one she had seen at least a dozen times before.

"Hey honey," Timothy called out for her attention.

"Yeah," she still didn't raise her head to look at him or turn off the TV.

"I think we need to talk." He uttered the scariest words in any relationship.

A few seconds later the TV screen went black, she turned it off. Cynthia stood up and joined him in the kitchen, a visibly worried look on her face. "Is everything okay?"

"I've been looking at our budget," he started out as he planned. Cynthia let out a brief sigh. Maybe she had been worried that he would have some worse news, an illness, an affair, anything else was more worrisome to Cynthia than their finances. She had always assumed everything was golden, that Timothy was able to fund any of her dreams. He hated to shatter that illusion, but that is what he needed to do.

He explained how they were spending more than they were bringing in. The house really was too much for them to afford. Her eyes seemed to glaze over as he pointed to the spreadsheets that he had printed out. She rubbed her temples as if she could massage the information into her brain.

"So, what does this all mean?"

It was as though she hadn't heard a thing he had just said.

"We need to cut back, and now. We need to log into our subscriptions tonight and cancel them. We probably need to cancel the cable, so enjoy those premium channels until the end of the month. And then we need to make an appointment to take your car in for an inspection and see what we need to do to get it ready to sell."

"Whoa, this is intense. Are we bankrupt?"

"No-" she cut him off before he could add the "not yet."

"Then why all these drastic measures? You're scaring me over nothing. We push back some of our plans to fix this place up. I guess we can show it off as-is. We just won't let anyone upstairs."

"What do you want to fix upstairs?"

She pushed on without acknowledging his question. "And you need to be home for dinner. No more dinner out each night. You should be home and eat with me. It is less expensive and then we can spend more time together."

"More time? I'm buried at work right now."

"Well, then you should be bringing in more to cover these costs. I'm salaried, I can't make anymore even if I would double my usual hours unless they decide to give me a raise or I find another job that pays more. I can start looking at that right away."

It was clear that Cynthia had made up her mind as to what changes were acceptable. Changes that Timothy could make and the one change that Cynthia already wanted, a raise. Any of his suggestions that applied to both of them were ignored. It was as though those options were laughable or so outrageous that she couldn't even acknowledge them.

Timothy began to shake his head. "We'll get through this together," she patted his hand with hers and scooped up Bentley who had been yipping at their heels for the entire conversation. "I'll heat up some dinner for you, okay?"

Timothy loosened the tie around his neck and plopped himself down on the couch. She handed him the microwave heated pizza with plastic-like cheese and a cold beer and she sat down next to him, turning the TV back on. "Come on and relax. It's Friday night."

He chewed with resentment. With each bite, he felt himself accepting Cynthia's version of reality. This was a fixable problem as long as Timothy made the sacrifices. It was only halfway through the slice that he remembered that he already had a dinner earlier; he was now just eating out of frustration.

They didn't speak much the rest of the night, although Cynthia offered commentary on the commercials and offered to clean his plate for him. He shuffled up the stairs when she did and changed for bed. "Don't worry about it tonight. Get a good night sleep. I'm glad you brought this up," she tried to gently rub his back and he lay facing the wall.

He didn't sleep well.

chapter 22

MELINDA RYECHIK, ON the other hand, had an excellent night sleep after a successful meeting with her boss. She and Jack had rehearsed what they would say to their respective bosses, expecting to get an earful of verbal grief if they truthfully answered about the reason they were leaving their jobs. "We might as well say we are going off and joining a cult, we need to tell them something that isn't untrue, but that won't throw up red flags."

"Or burn any bridges," Melinda had interjected into their rehearsals.

Jack smirked. He was okay to take every professional and personal bridge and light it on fire if needed. *Why stay connected to people who only want to hold you back?* This was a question he had once asked Melinda. She was with him, but wasn't nearly as prepared as he was to leave everyone and everything behind, until now. As they rehearsed, he conceded her point, acknowledging that they did need a fallback plan, in case everything they had been working towards fell apart.

Having thoroughly rehearsed, Melinda had been prepared for every outcome of her meeting. She was even prepared for the pleasant acceptance that her boss expressed.

"Well, we are sorry to see you go. Is there any way we could get you to stay on?" he had slumped back in his chair when she gave him the news that she would be vacating her position in short order. His face, stretched out from years of consuming excess calories with nowhere else to go, was more pink that his flamboyantly salmon button-down shirt, evidence of a weekend spent baking outside. Just the sight of him made her lips parch and her cheeks blanch with the sting of sun-poisoning.

"No," she offered a finite response before continuing with the socially required niceties. "I, of course, enjoyed my time here, but I'd ready for my next-"

"Adventure?" he interjected, man-terrupting in true form.

"Hmmm, more like a vocation," she had to correct him. Melinda couldn't let him usurp her glorious moment by cutting her off and trying to guess what was really on her mind.

Her boss nodded. Immediately thoughts of run down, mud packed hovels teaming with toothless children filled his mind. Missionary work, her calling. His imagination went the route that most would think of at the word: vocation.

Seeing him mull over the reason given for her departure Melinda quickly added, "Well, it means a lot to me, and to Jack."

Accepting her words and knowing that he would have a few more weeks to pry, he decided that it was time to conclude their conversation. "I wish you both the best of luck. But, if you need some cash, give me a call, we can always use freelancers."

"Will do."

As she left she felt her chest tighten. This was it. The last cord to cut before the vast "after." The time that would be filled... how? Every moment has been leading to the Big Day. But after that, it was all a big void. If everything went according to plan on the day of, they would be on the road, moving around each day, living off as little as possible to make their resources last as long as they could. *But, it will be worth it*, she thought to herself as she pictured that big moment.

chapter **23**

BEFORE TIMOTHY LEFT for work on that Saturday morning, Cynthia did her best to protest. He had left the office so late the previous evening they didn't really get a night together.

"No, I need to go in. There is work to be done and I need to bill these hours."

"Can't we set up a home-office for you?"

"We can't afford to do that right now," he was so frustrated he didn't even acknowledge that she was trying to help him out. He was always stressed; she hadn't seen him smile or ease up all summer.

"I'll be back tonight. Please don't go shopping today, okay?"

So not only was he going to dismiss her ideas, he was going to reduce her to just a vapid woman who spent all of her time shopping. "I wasn't planning on it," she responded to him, clearly miffed. *Although now it sounds like a great idea*, she thought to herself.

"Just remember our talk last night, we can dig out of this together, but we both have to be committed to it."

After he left, she was fuming. Like this problem was all her fault. He was the one who signed for the mortgage, he was the one who took the second loan to pay for his car. *But I did get a wedding loan that he doesn't know anything about*, the honest little angel in her brain chimed in. *Shut it*, the devil on her shoulder snapped back.

She knew exactly what she needed to cool down; she needed a long walk in a brightly-lit place. A positive place where no one ever has any worries and she can be around her favorite things. She needed a trip to the mall.

Cynthia arrived at the mall with the same distress one would expect to see on a sinner arriving at a mid-week mass. She needed the relief of escape, she needed her routine: starting at her favorite lingerie store, then the four anchor stores in the mall, followed by her favorite specialty shops, and finally a stop at Starbucks. She would sip her caramel whipped treat with the slow reverence of a Catholic receiving the blood of Christ.

She was one of the freest people in the world. A middle-class white woman in America, she was the benefactor of a lifetime of advantage and opportunity. She was more free than a woman in Tehran or Bangladesh. She had the means to feed herself and her family, she could dress and speak as she pleased. She could work and travel without any reasonable fear of attack. She was so free, that she indebted and enslaved herself to clothes, cars, food, and Facebook. Youth may be wasted on the young, but freedom is squandered on the privileged.

At the mall, she eyed the designer shoes in the department store. The floors were cream marble, the shelves gilded, making each color on the leather handbags and satin high heels pop as her eyes covetously pass across each of them.

Erik had popped over to her desk again to have a little chat the day before. He must have enjoyed his little stunt, she saw it for what it was.

He tapped her on the shoulder, "Hey, I need your opinion!"

Cynthia expected a question on an account or perhaps professional advice that she would be able to offer. Instead, he pulled two boxes out of a thick bag, the kind of thick shiny plastic that is the hallmark of a productive shopping trip with braided handles and thick cardboard at the bottom to maintain the shape of the bag even when it is empty.

"What do you think?" he opened the two boxes, each containing a different but equally expensive pair of high heels. This interaction felt contrived from the outset, but Cynthia was already picking up the shoes and turning them over for a more careful inspection.

"These shoes are gorgeous!" She wasn't able to tell him that they were too big for her feet. She didn't know why she automatically assumed that they were for her, but in her mind, she was already picking out which of her dresses she could wear them with.

"You think? They certainly cost enough. But, as a woman, which one would you want more?"

After an appraisal, she noticed that the black pair was plain, classic, but was clearly the more expensive pair with the signature red patent leather sole. The other was a nude with subtle sparkles along the heel. The second pair was from an equally prestigious designer, but that wasn't as easy to identify to the naked eye.

"The black pair. Everyone knows what this red means," Cynthia pointed to her choice and rubbed her thumb against her forefingers, indicating the money that was spent on the shoes was what mattered.

"I was thinking the black pair because black goes with everything. But I know she already has quite a few pairs of black heels."

Cynthia was picturing her lavender party dress with the addition of the black heels when Erik's comment popped her fantasy as though it were a delicate soap bubble.

"Pardon?"

"My girlfriend, she already has a lot of black heels. I don't know much about fashion, but I know those red soles are a big deal, right?"

Suddenly very uninterested, Cynthia retorted, "Honestly once she sees the label on the box she won't really care what's in it."

Erik packed up the first box with the nude shoes. "Well, I figure I can always show her both but let her know she can only keep one. These were really expensive."

"You've already purchased them though, might as well keep 'em," Cynthia returned to her work.

"I guess," Erik placed the second box back in the bag. "Thanks for your help," he smiled with pride that he had picked the correct designers. Or perhaps he was gloating at his ability to pay for both without a second thought. Or perhaps he was smug that he had been able to get under Cynthia's skin, a change-up from the usual.

"Anytime," Cynthia turned her head and smiled. "But maybe check her size again. Those looked really big," a subtle dig was enough to make her feel like she got the last word in. Cynthia had never even met this woman and already she was jealous of her. This woman got the new romance and excitement of dates and gifts and the potential for a proposal. Timothy had never purchased her anything that extravagant (although the honest voice within her head chimed in that he had just bought her a house). With his latest kick about saving and trying to budget better, there would be no way that he would let her buy shoes like that, not even the well-done knock-offs.

Cynthia relived the humiliation of that moment when Erik walked away as she eyed the shoes in the store. In his subtle gesture, he made it clear that he was willing to spoil the woman he was with, the woman who she would never be. Feeling this self-repulsion as though it were fresh, she grabbed the bright blue satin heels in front of her with the rhinestone cluster on the heel.

She assured herself that she would only try them on, to see how they looked. They were so outrageously expensive that she could never think of purchasing them. But they fit perfectly, no need for the thin cork-layers that she had to shove into her other heels. *They would go nicely with at least a dozen of my outfits*, she thought as she eyed them from multiple angles in the dressing room mirror. She liked how they made her backside perk up when she strained her neck to see her own rear-view.

She pictured how great she would feel walking into work on Monday with these shoes on, striding right past Erik who would never have the fashion sense to pick these beauties. Maybe he had some sick obsession with her and wanted his girlfriend to wear the shoes that Cynthia selected, maybe he even would picture her face when they made love after she happily tried them on for him. *Gross*, she rolled her eyes at the thought of his sick infatuation with her, a married woman.

She stepped out of the heels and gently placed them back in the box. Sad to see them stay at the store she put on her flats and grabbed her purse, her eyes catching the wear along the seam that held the leather handle together. *Great, another thing that I can't replace.* Timothy's budget was already unmanageable.

As she walked out of the carpeted dressing room, a feeling she usually associated with glee and an eager excitement to make her purchase, she frowned as she passed the attendant. She handed over the box with a sigh.

"Didn't fit huh? I can see if we have these in a different size."

"Oh no, they fit perfectly, but they're just a bit out of my budget for now. Maybe when they go on sale," Cynthia's resolve was fading but she felt proud of herself for resisting. She continued walking until she heard, "Wait!"

Turning she saw the young attendant with her bright red hair and straight cut bangs waving her to come back. "There is a blue tag on the bottom, that means these are 20% off!"

"20% off!?" Cynthia did the mental math quickly, they were still way out of range, but these shoes fit her perfectly. If she didn't buy them now, then surely someone else would. The sale price was a sign, a divination from on-high, she needed to own these shoes.

After a few moments to complete the transaction, Cynthia bounced out of the store, swinging her big structured bag, and smiling like a satisfied child. She had her purchase. Timothy would be at work all day; she could easily add the shoes to the closet without him even noticing.

To complete her trip to the mall she popped into her favorite coffee shop. This time she would just be redeeming her loyalty card for her free latte that she earned after purchasing 10 others.

The hum of the coffee roaster was so ever-present that you almost forgot it was there. The ritual was complete, she entered the store, found the item, made the purchase, and now she would come down from her thrilling high with the sugar-filled delicacy that was being hand-made just for her.

She sat at one of the bistro tables outside of the coffee shop, looking at the other shoppers as they strolled by, a promenade of other purchases made. Single women marching towards the exit, heads held high with pride as multiple brightly colored bags swung from their arms. Men, not much older than her, fixated on the small boxes they had just procured that contained their newest gadgets. She was one of them. *See, this is normal. And I saved money on the shoes and didn't even have to pay for the coffee. I'm already saving us money.*

As she finished taking a sip of her latte, she noticed a man staring at her. Had she been muttering that last thought aloud, talking to herself? He continued to look at her, and she recognized the smirk on his face. He was checking her out. She was an attractive woman out alone at the mall, why shouldn't he think that she might be available? She smiled and pushed her hair back behind her shoulder, a subtle acknowledgment of her admirer, inviting him to have a longer look. After a few moments passed, she continued to sip her coffee, now more deliberate and slow, to let this flirtation linger.

But, of course, there were no witnesses to the beautiful moment that she was trying to savor. No one would smile with anticipation as their attraction brought them exponentially closer like planets swirling closer and closer to the event horizon of a black hole. No cameras were rolling to broadcast the triumph of Cynthia's spirit. And that is what it was. In that moment, she was the center of this man's attention. The world slipped away. Timothy faded back to the recesses of her memory. Yes, Timothy was her husband, but she felt destined for something more. A more exciting love, one that would leave her suspended in a constant free-fall. That is what each woman deserved right?

Cynthia had spent so long convincing herself that she was both a great and devoted wife (with little evidence to support that claim) and infinitely tempting and desired by all men. The latter may have been true, at least in the case of Erik, but she was most definitely not a devoted and faithful wife. She had been edging the line with her flirtations, but now she was inviting this attention. It crossed a line. Even though Timothy had failed to secure her all of the things she desired, and he didn't think they could afford booking the cruise she wanted, he was working extra hours to cover their costs. Cynthia was stubborn in her ways. She needed the perfect marriage, with elegant anniversary gifts, a boy and girl born within an appropriate amount of time. But she also needed the constant excitement of something big happening, she needed to have a big event on the horizon, not just more of the same. She would never be content to have just enough, she needed more.

chapter 24

THE RYECHIKS LEFT before anyone was awake, sneaking away in the silence of the morning, their only witnesses the beads of dew gathering on the grass and the pair of stray cats caught in their headlights. Their van rolled silently through the neighborhood, out to the main road, and onto the highway without much other traffic. Their holiday weekend was starting without a hitch, which was a good sign. This was their practice run weekend. If things didn't go well, they may have to push back *the date*. While everyone else was planning to spend the holiday of American Independence hosting parties in their mansions that kept them enslaved to decades of hard work, the Ryechiks were about to do a clean run-through of the plan that would free them from all of that.

The Fourth of July holiday weekend appeared abruptly. The Lawsons had little time to prepare their home for the party Cynthia had been worrying over.

Only Timothy's family and some close friends were invited. Timothy extended the invitation to Dan and his family, but they were going out of town. He sent a text over to Jack Ryechik, who informed him that he and Melinda had other plans.

Cynthia spent the morning cleaning and preparing elaborate recipes that were standard fare with a twist. She was not thrilled with the upstairs so she made a point to exclude that for her tours, calling it a work-in-progress. She hung red, white, and blue cray-paper streamers across the staircase to bar anyone from venturing onto the second floor.

Half of the cul-de-sac cleared out for trips to see family. The other half invited people over to barbecues making it easy for the oversized trucks,

SUVs, and minivans to flood the curbs and make the road difficult to navigate. At noon, their guests began to arrive, much to Cynthia's frustration. She had asked people to arrive in the early afternoon, not at noon. She rolled her eyes as she started to gather drinks from the refrigerator and switched to her hostess' smile when she handed the early-arrivers their beverages.

Timothy tended to his family, per Cynthia's request, so that she could focus on getting all of the food prepared. Arriving on time, Henrietta greeted Cynthia and asked where she should put the wine that she brought. A kind housewarming gift to anyone else, Cynthia sighed and said, "I'll find a place for it," as she grimaced at the label. *Really, a French wine on the fourth of July? Shouldn't you be on the wagon honey?*

The pair of women hadn't spoken since the *incident* earlier that summer and Cynthia shut down each of Timothy's updates on Henri's legal problems with a quick, "well crime doesn't pay," platitude that sounded more terse each time she uttered it.

Sensing the disdain coming from her hostess, Henrietta politely excused herself and spent most of the evening in a deck chair facing the pond with her cell phone in-hand. She spoke with Timothy about the information he had requested and quickly slipped him a piece of paper with the contact for a private investigator she had once hired to trail her philandering ex-husband. Timothy nervously pocketed the information, regretting that he had even asked about it, while also relieved that he had an option now.

Henrietta was discrete and didn't pry any further, her cousin had already disclosed his concerns to her the previous day in his office about Cynthia's spending and his suspicions of infidelity. Henrietta wasn't surprised and found this to be inevitable, ever since she saw Cynthia eyeing up wedding dresses and more focused on the sequin count than her cousin's input on their wedding. But, she kept her mouth shut, no need to rub his nose in it.

The remainder of the guests arrived, some good friends of Cynthia's flooded the back patio with their raucous discussions and off-color jokes. They had their disposable trendy red cups as they greedily piled food onto their disposable plates. They photographed quick moments for disposable social affirmations and pings on their phones. They had disposable conversations about the vehicles they planned to upgrade and the relationships they had eulogized with merciless details about their paramours.

And where did it all go? These single serving items. These disposable cups. The individually wrapped snacks, the cola cans, the coffee cups, the beer bottles, the wrappers, the cellophane, the oil, the trash? To the local landfill, of course, smoldering like a mountain alive with noxious gases, the outer visible scar. Because that's what garbage is. A scar. It is a bleeding wound, the visible evidence of the violence we as parasites inflict on the Earth. But, don't count her out, don't assume that she is a timid victim. She still has her sweet revenge coming, equal in measure.

After the sun set behind the trees, the mosquitos descended in full force, driving the guests inside for refuge in the crisp air-conditioned family room. Timothy flipped on one of the cable channels that had a movie marathon playing as everyone began to nibble on chips and finish their beers. Cynthia went outside with Bentley to let him have his evening bathroom visit, carrying a flashlight to make sure she didn't step in any of his droppings.

The day had gone well, but their guests hadn't seemed to be as impressed by the house as she had hoped they would be. She was decorating that huge house all by herself, with Timothy working late nights and weekends. Of course, her father-in-law only wanted to discuss business and Henri was never any fun at all. Cynthia had been happy to see her friends posting photos of the dinner spread and tagging her in the images.

As Bentley made his way around the edge of the lawn, Cynthia focused her eyes on the gray exterior of the Ryechik's house. They had declined an invitation to attend to the Lawson's barbecue because they would be 'out of town.' After everything that she had learned about the Mahaskals and the Ryechiks, she was morbidly curious and absolutely certain that she might find something amiss in their house. Checking that no one from inside her own house was peering into the yard she quickly scooped up Bentley and made her way across the backyard.

Gently climbing the stairs to the back porch as lightly as she could, she felt like a true rebel. *I hope I don't get caught.* She tried to peer in through the glass, but the house was pitch black. Expecting it to be locked she touched her fingertips to the handle and felt it easily give way. *They didn't lock the back door.* She checked to her left and right and even turned around, making sure there were no canoers on the pond, no witnesses, and she slipped into the pitch-black void that was the Ryechik household.

As she remembered, the downstairs was mostly empty but it seemed to be missing even more items. The kitchen counter was completely bare, but perhaps Melinda liked to store each of their appliances when not using them. Cynthia made her way through the first floor and quickly headed upstairs. The spare rooms were completely empty except for one.

It appeared to be an office with a simple metal frame desk, a pair of plastic rolling chairs, and a large computer monitor. There was a corkboard above the desk featuring several pictures of Jack and Melinda on many different vacations. They looked hot and sweaty but they were smiling, laughing even, in these pictures. Cynthia envied them for a moment, wishing that she and Timothy could get away to an island and perhaps rekindle their spark.

This fantasy ended when her eyes passed over the hanging calendar next to the corkboard with the month of July marked up. The first three days had hash-marks through them and the holiday weekend was high-lighted in red marker "TRIAL RUN." As her eyes began to process the words, she saw that the following weekend had a large red "X" on Friday. *They were going to do something the following week and whatever it was they were practicing it right now.*

She was leaning closer and closer to the calendar, as if it might reveal some new secrets if she could only see it within millimeters of her eyes. She felt the edge of the desk jab into her thigh; she let out a muted "hmph" of frustrated pain. She looked down at the desk and saw a key, one of those small ones with the square top that was so easy to identify as the desk key.

What would they be keeping locked up? Cynthia wondered. Theories began to fly around her head. Evidence that they killed the Mahaskals. Details for whatever this trial run really is about. The possibilities were limitless. With a quick action, she unlocked and slid the top-drawer open, the castors rolling silently, smoothly. The desk really did have a very sleek design. The drawer contained some pencils, a few business cards, and a short stack of drawings. The first few were schematics, or blueprints maybe. The paper was so thin she could see right through it and knew enough to realize that she would never be able to decipher the details laid out. The next few had some feathers drawn with an expert hand, Melinda's no doubt.

The final one had a series of words drawn and re-drawn, covering the page. "Combatting the ENEMIES of PEACE." "Fighting the ENEMIES of PEACE." Drawn out in block text and cursive. Tested many times and in many styles. Was this their mantra? Were they affiliated with some paramilitary group? Combat? Fighting?

Then, Cynthia remembered something. It all clicked into place. *How to spot the terrorist next-door.*

With her adrenaline pumping, she began to worry that she should leave immediately. *What if the Ryechiks came home early? What if Timothy came looking for her AND then the Ryechiks came home early?*

There was no way to explain herself, but surely what she had uncovered was enough to confirm her suspicions. The papers were put back in the drawer, the desk locked, the key set on the corner of the desk.

She marched down the stairs quickly, squeezing Bentley as she went. Passing by the garage door, she stopped and turned back. Maybe she should check in there too, maybe whatever they were practicing this weekend may have some evidence in the garage. She fixed the flashlight on the door knob and placed Bentley on the ground, keeping his leash tight around her wrist. She reached for the door knob and heard her name.

"Cynthia!"

She could hear Timothy outside; she must have worried him being gone so long. She clicked off the flashlight and kept moving towards the back porch, leaving the garage undisturbed. She would never know for sure what was, or wasn't in there that night. If she had opened it, she would have seen a vast slab of concrete and empty shelves. The garage was empty too, but Cynthia would never confirm that with her own eyes.

Cynthia rejoined the party just as the first of the fireworks exploded over the pond.

"Where were you?" Timothy asked, his mouth a little too close to Cynthia's face, the heavy scent of beer on his breath inflaming her nostrils.

"Just taking Bentley for his walk," Cynthia shrugged, keeping in mind to make herself appear calm. She had to wait until the guests left to tell him. For those few moments, as Bentley trembled in her arms at the loud explosions in the sky, she enjoyed Timothy's drunk and greedy hands on her hip, reminding her of their more invigorating days together. She couldn't help but peer over her shoulder to check that the house next door was still dark, no one was watching her from an upstairs window, no one was menacingly studying her, aware of her intrusion and calculating revenge.

The house vacated and the dishwasher full, the Lawsons retreated to their master bedroom. Timothy had one thing on his mind and it was not sleeping. Cynthia also had one thing on her mind, and it was not at all what Timothy was thinking of. As she began to unpin her earrings and remove her hair clips, she described what she found in the Ryechik's house to Timothy. Flabbergasted by her admission, Timothy was quickly turned-off and sat on their bed, head in hands, unable to process this new information.

"Why in the world would you go in there?"

"We've both had our suspicions!" Cynthia was on the defensive now.

"What suspicions?" The woman standing before him was starting to look like a stranger, like she was a truly deranged person.

"You're the one who mentioned that white van,"

"Yeah, so,"

"So, you clearly thought something was amiss, or else you wouldn't have mentioned it."

"I still think you are making more out of it than there is." Timothy tried to dismiss her concerns, he could indulge her other far-fetched fantasies of having their wedding featured in national magazines (which never panned out), but this was a whole new level.

"Don't you get it? They have sold off all of their possessions because they are either going to be on the run or in jail after next week. That is a documented behavior of suicide missions."

Timothy was silent, Cynthia was encouraged by this when she should have realized that she had already said too much. "Also, the 9/11 hijackers did trial runs the week before the attacks, another documented behavior."

"Yeah, or they are just going camping again next weekend."

"And what happened to the Mahaskals? They were close friends and then they disappear. No one saw them after Tyler and Jack had that argument."

"You don't even know if it was an argument."

"I still think we should alert somebody. Maybe I am wrong, but what if I am right? What if they are planning something?" Her words were prophetic, and perhaps if Timothy had known how they would meet their end he might have insisted that she say something. But he brushed off her words, believing in the improbability of her accusations.

"Jack is a nice guy, we get along. I think I would know if our next-door neighbors were some kind of homegrown radicals." Giving in to her theories for a second, Timothy just couldn't place the two opposing images of Jack in his mind.

"But that is what they always say after the fact, 'he seemed so nice, I had no idea he was about to blow up a school!'" Her voice hit a shrill note, her words becoming more ragged and frantic, needing to be heard.

"Who is they?"

"They, the media, their friends, and family. All so shocked, but someone had to have known something. I'm telling you those people are weird. The way they act and dress, even the way they talk. *'No, I don't mean what you do for money, what do you do?'*" she mocked Jack's insightful question from their first dinner together.

"Well in a week, you will see that this is all just silliness. I bet you'll forget most of this by tomorrow." Timothy kissed her on the forehead and tucked himself into bed, rolling over so that he faced the wall. The conversation was over. He wouldn't be listening to anymore of her hysterics.

Cynthia pressed on, "I think the Mahaskals were, in fact, close with the Ryechiks, and they found something out and they," she paused before enunciating each word, "took care of them."

"Took care of them? Seriously? You need to stop watching whatever shows are making you think this is normal. It's not. And now you're going to have more nightmares tonight." Exhausted, Timothy got up from the bed grabbing his pillow. He didn't want to have any more arguments tonight or any more imagined problems to solve for his wife.

"Timothy, this is for real. Don't they give you a weird vibe?" She was pleading with him not to leave, her words may not have said it, but the tears threatening to spill over her eyes were shouting it to the back of his head.

"I'm done talking about this. I'm sleeping on the couch tonight." He shut the door behind him with a loud click, Cynthia stood by the bed abandoned. Just another crazy woman with her crazy ideas and a man who wouldn't listen to her.

chapter 25

IN THE STILL and quiet emptiness of the living room, Jack Ryechik reclined in the fold-up camping chair that was one of three remaining items in the entire downstairs of their house. The water-resistant fabric gave enough smooth support to prevent injury to his back, but not enough lumbar support to sit comfortably for too long. On that quiet Monday morning, Melinda was upstairs making her own final preparations. She was picking out the exact outfit she intended to wear for the big day. It seemed like such a trivial detail, but she was fixated on finding the perfect combination from her recently reduced wardrobe.

Jack could hear her shuffling about upstairs as he took in the vast white emptiness of the walls, bare and completely smooth. Having been recently painted bright white, they were almost blinding as the sun filtered through the opened windows and splashed across vast bands of the exposed walls.

His cell phone rang and the standard chimes sounded off. He picked up the flip-phone from a small box that had served as a make-shift coffee table between the two camp chairs set up in the living room.

"Hello," he answered firmly, feeling a slight apprehension every time, he saw an incoming call from that number. *Would it be good news or bad? Would there be some unforeseen circumstance that would cause a delay or require additional funds to handle?*

The voice on the other end was cheery, effusive. Jack could never match the level of this man's verbal enthusiasm. Maybe the stress had been wearing on him too much, there were so many details to plan, so many final items to put in place. He was sure he would miss something and that unsettled him.

After the man finished talking Jack responded with some questions. "Okay, and the cash will be available when?"

The man's response was acceptable. He would take his own cut, for sure, but there would still be more than enough for the Ryechiks to live on after they took off.

"And the date hasn't changed?"

Again, a positive answer. Jack began to feel slightly more relaxed. No big last-minute changes; the plan was being executed so well. There was still a nagging feeling that he was missing something, but perhaps if he couldn't remember what that thing was, it wasn't that important after all.

The conversation concluded and Jack flipped the phone shut. He grabbed his laptop from the space beneath his folding chair. He updated the already overly-detailed and methodical notes on his multi-tabbed Excel document. He knew that most people would see him and his wife as crazy, as fanatical, but he was compelled to complete this task. The rest of his life was at stake.

chapter **26**

CYNTHIA'S CONSTERNATION EARLY on in the week paid off with a job interview on Friday. Having an outfit to select and questions to practice, she mostly forgot about the Ryechiks and whatever they may or may not have been planning.

On Thursday, less than 24 hours before her interview, and less than 36 hours before the Ryechiks would indeed execute on their plan, Cynthia chatted with Erik about the interview over coffee. Her plan was to leverage an offer for more money. The company that had responded to her application was a fabrication and manufacturing outfit located closer to her home, but away from the excitement of the downtown hustle and bustle. Erik offered her some advice based on his experience conducting interviews.

Cynthia took notes and paid for Erik's coffee to thank him for his help. Their friendship was strained ever since he began to flaunt his new relationship. Cynthia was happy to see that they could continue to be friends, even though it was clear that he had moved past his idle fixation on her. Did she look normal to him now, the way a beautiful painting begins to seem commonplace after passing it day after day?

"Thank you for your help, I'm so nervous about the interview," Cynthia admitted as she fiddled with the empty straw wrapper in front of her.

"Anytime, although it will be a bummer if you leave," Erik tried to make eye contact with her as he admitted one small sentiment whereas he intended to express a million other nuanced feelings.

"If all goes according to plan, I can get a raise and stay," Cynthia looked up and smiled as though her plan would all come together. All of her little schemes worked out, she got the best wedding ever by taking out the loan she needed, she got the best house ever, she got exactly what she wanted.

"Let's hope so," Erik proffered, his experience told him that tactic usually didn't work unless the employee could actually walk away. "What if your boss says she won't counter? What if it is too much?"

"Hmm, I doubt it. She needs me on the team to survive, no one else does as much as me," the words tasted like lies on her tongue, but she washed away the flavor with her iced coffee drink.

"Ok," Erik nodded, clearly Cynthia was not getting his point. There were large gaping flaws in her plan. "What if you actually want this job? What if they make you a great offer?"

"Eh, I'm not excited about the idea of working in a *plant*." She emphasized the word and mashed up the vowel sound in her mouth to elongate it and give it a mid-western sound that was exaggerated and unappealing.

"Then maybe don't do the interview," Erik tried to educate Cynthia.

Shocked and betrayed by the one man left in her life who had yet to patronize her, Cynthia rolled her eyes. Timothy would never tell her not to do the interview, Timothy would have never told her to give up. Timothy had also not said a word when she told him that she landed the interview and had offered no help. The man that she had married was two very different people to her at all times. In one part of her mind, he was a kind husband who didn't cheat, who bought her a fancy house, and tried to please her. He never complained when she took too long to get ready and he would rub her back whenever she got sick. In the other part of her mind, he was constantly ignoring her, unable to understand her truest and most deep-seeded need for attention. He didn't buy her gifts 'just because', he scoffed at the idea of a European vacation. He worked such long hours that she hardly ever saw him anymore. In that moment, Timothy was all these things to her, a savior from a single life where she would be stuck dealing with men like Erik all the time, but also the ultimate let down that she was off the market, sworn to love a man who was no longer excited by her.

"Well, if I get the job and it is more money, I'm either going to leverage for more money here or I'll make more money there. Either way, we'll be able to save up for a second honeymoon in Europe." Cynthia threw out the words "we" and "honeymoon" as though they would be spears directly into Erik's psyche. She hoped that they would cause the damage that she hoped for; she wanted to see him wince. Instead, he shrugged, *he must be masking his pain well*. Cynthia had to believe that. Otherwise, he truly didn't care and then she would be left in that massive empty house all alone for the rest of her life.

They finished by exchanging bits about their worst interview horror stories. The conversation reverted back to their usual back and forth, the easy and charming repartee that had first drawn Cynthia to Erik.

All along her drive home, Cynthia tried on different outfits in her mind, trying to picture which elements from her wardrobe would be best for the interview. She wanted to look polished and professional, but the locale might require something more perfunctory and normal, a mainstream look might be less threatening. She considered her black skirt, but dismissed it remembering how she felt the last time she wore it: puffy and pudgy. She considered the gray skirt instead, one that was structured and would go well with her green blouse. After thinking through each of her outfits, she settled on a dress. Of course, she would still try on her top three options that evening for Timothy. She sent him a text as she sat at a red light, hoping to entice him with the promise of a fashion show for the interview, and then perhaps a look or two from her lingerie collection, just for Timothy.

When she pulled into the driveway at 501 Hurley Pond she saw the plain white van in the driveway at the Ryechiks. She remembered the big red circle drawn on their calendar for tomorrow, Friday. *Could the white van be part of whatever they were rehearsing?*

Before her brain could connect the white van with whatever she knew Jack and Melinda were planning and her intense suspicion of them, her phone buzzed, preventing her from making the mental leaps necessary to think that they would be executing a dangerous plan, or a safe plan, or any plan. She was distracted and excited to respond to texts from her husband.

PART 4

Anger

Why Brownlee Left
BY PAUL MULDOON
"Why Brownlee left, and where he went,
Is a mystery even now.
For if a man should have been content
It was him…"

chapter 27

THE NEXT MORNING when Timothy left for work, he noticed the white van in his neighbor's driveway well past the hour when he would have usually left for work. The thought struck him as odd, but he quickly wiped it from his mind. Cynthia's interview was that afternoon. She would get the job, she would get a raise, they would start to eat away at all the debt. It would take some time, but they would do it.

Daydreaming on his drive in, Timothy began to update the checkboxes of the newly constructed budget in his mind. If she had a shorter commute, then the cost for gas would also go down, and perhaps insurance as well. She could go home for lunch to play with Bentley and then they could stop using the doggy day-care service that seemed to be as expensive as a private school for human children.

When he arrived at work, he was completely convinced that he and Cynthia would be out of their dire financial situation within the next few months, easily. He sorted through all of the documentation that he had printed out and itemized each credit card that they had, the balance due, the interest. He tallied up the balances on their car loans. Cynthia would get the job, they would pay off the first things that they could. Everything would work out.

A knock at his office door announced that Henri was waiting to come in. She smiled and closed the door behind her before she spoke.

"Dad is so mad at me," she confessed as she collapsed into Timothy's side chair.

"Well, you had to tell him. He knows every judge in the county," Timothy had tried his best to coach her over the past week. Her DUI lawyer had advised her to plead guilty to the charge and beg forgiveness to get the minimum possible sentence. Being a Lawson had advantages and this was her first offense. They both knew that her father could (and would) call in a few favors to make sure she was treated in the most preferential way possible.

Henri nodded silently as they both heard the elder Lawsons roaring from Randolph's office. The walls were solid so they were surely in a screaming match. The cousins eyed each other sheepishly, they felt like insolent children who had been banished to their bedroom while the adults ranted about their latest antics.

"He got so red in the face, Timothy," she shook her head and tried her best to fight off the tears that were brimming in her eyes. Her face turned hot pink again, like it had on the night of her arrest.

"It's okay. You're allowed to make mistakes, Henri. He just wants to see that you learn from it." Timothy reached across the papers on his desk to touch her hand. As his own hand receded from hers, he moved the financial statements and turned them over. He didn't want Henri to know that he had screwed up too. He didn't want to tell her that his own father had done some string-pulling to keep him from going bankrupt within months of buying a new home. He could handle the rest of the family being upset with Henri, but he couldn't yet admit the depth of his own failure. It was okay for Henri to know that he and Cynthia weren't getting along. But he couldn't admit that he had made financial mistakes as well, avoidable and completely unnecessary financial mistakes.

She sat quietly and collected herself. After a moment, she stood and left the room, offering a "thank you," before she left. Timothy didn't want to admit it, but his life was potentially just a few months away from where Henri was: rock bottom. If things didn't turn around financially, if Cynthia didn't help to get their finances back in order, if Kellyanne winked at him again in that certain way, he could see where he was headed: divorce, debt, destruction. As much as he pitied his cousin, he was certain he did not want to end up like her, even if that was a harsh assessment.

After lunch at the sports bar where his favorite someone was pulling a mid-day shift, Timothy arrived back at the office to see both his father and uncle had left early to get a jump on their weekend. Henri left a note on his door stating that she was planning on going home, putting her car keys in the freezer, and finishing a bottle of wine to help her forget the day.

He had the office to himself. He quickly thought of texting Kellyanne, inviting her to see the office. But he knew what his motive was and he wanted to avoid that temptation as long as he could. Besides, he had just eaten, his message would have been completely transparent and he didn't want to risk being rejected.

Once he sat down at his desk, he saw that he had two missed calls. Both callers had left voicemails, one was their credit card company inquiring into the missed payments. The other was David Quinten, again, from the bank, informing him that in the case of a missed payment the bank was entitled to start proceedings to reclaim the home. Because of his status as a preferred member of the bank, they would give him one more month. That meant that his father and uncle were preferred members, and he was getting a pass because of their name.

With these troubles on his mind, he decided to bite the bullet and look at his credit score, that once-a-year free report from multiple sources, and it was bad. How had he even qualified for a mortgage? Shouldn't having a mortgage help his credit? Maybe the mortgage was hurting his credit? This led to a tailspin where he spent all afternoon pouring over every bank statement and credit card bill.

He was overwhelmed and eager to turn away from the computer and ignore the mountain of financial trouble, a mountain that was moving, rumbling his way, thundering down the driveway, shuttering the windows. He noticed that there was one item out of place as well, which made him feel hopeful that their score would improve, while simultaneously making him worry that their identities had been stolen and used to take out a loan.

An outstanding $20,000 loan with $17,000 remaining in principle was taken out under Cynthia's name and was showing on one of the three credit reports under Timothy's name as well. He didn't mention it to Cynthia, not yet. He had only just discovered it and he didn't want her to worry or panic until he had more information.

They would need to take better care of their personal data. After all, his was a household name, well-known from those commercials. It was best to come to Cynthia with a plan. But, even once that line-item was resolved, they still had their remaining bills to worry about.

He needed her to curb her spending, he needed her to text him and say that she had been offered that higher paying job to continue to make ends meet.

He thought about their last discussion on the topic and knew that he couldn't say that to Cynthia with a straight face. It was his responsibility, and he had OK-ed each purchase, he was complicit, and for some of the loans, he was entirely responsible. *One thing at a time*, he reminded himself. *Take care of this erroneous personal loan and then onto the next item to pay off.*

He almost laughed to himself thinking how silly it was that anyone could think that Cynthia would take out a personal loan. She would rather face public ridicule than admit she didn't have the cash on hand to buy anything. Besides, it showed that the loan started a few months before their wedding; Cynthia was too busy with color schemes and tastings to think about the necessary paperwork to start a loan.

A sinister thought crossed his mind, *what if she did take out the loan?* If she was hiding this from him, a $20,000 lie, what else could she be hiding? He shook his head as if that could get that idea out of his mind, as if that could erase the first glimmer of betrayal. Cynthia was many things, but she would never lie that big. She was one for small little lies, telling Henri that she liked her outfit when it was clear that she didn't care for it. Telling people that their dogs looked precious, even though she was whole-heartedly sure that Bentley was the only cute puppy on the planet. Cynthia didn't do big lies like that. And if she was lying about this, what else was he in the dark on? It was a dark hole that he didn't want to fall down.

Trying to convince himself that his wife could never do such a thing, he shot her a quick text wishing her good luck at the interview. She should have already been there by now, which meant he should have sent that text at least an hour ago. *Better late than never*, he told himself.

Putting aside his personal finances and the worry about the (potentially) false loan on their credit, Timothy refocused on the Hydroline case. They would start litigation within the next two weeks and he wanted the case to be perfect, no hiccups, no surprises.

He plunged into the world of his work and hardly realized that two hours had passed when his phone buzzed. He had a new text from Cynthia; he was excited and nervous to see what she would say. How long had it been since he had last felt that way about something as small as a text from her?

"I got it!" was all that the text read. Timothy could barely believe what he was seeing. Yes, she had the offer, now they could put his plan into action.

"I knew you could do it!" he shot off quickly. "Let's do dinner tonight to celebrate," he followed up immediately. It was still early, not even four in the afternoon yet, but the rest of the office had cleared out. Surely, this occasion warranted an early departure.

Cynthia responded quickly with several smiling face emojis and two wine glass emojis. He could tell she was excited, and why wouldn't she be. Since she had told her boss that she had a doctor's appointment, she didn't have to return to work that afternoon. They could both begin to celebrate right away.

On his was down to the car he thumbed through his wallet, he had spent the last of his cash on lunch. Given the additional messages from the bank and the credit card companies, he didn't want to risk trying to pay for dinner with a card and be declined. Not in front of Cynthia, not in front of anyone. He decided to do the drive-through ATM on the way home. When he pulled up into the stile, after idling for some twenty minutes, he was informed that his account was overdrawn. The bank had some policy about removing funds from your checking and savings account to cover your mortgage if you were late. It kept him from being foreclosed on, but also meant he had no option to pay for dinner.

What would Cynthia say? He had already made the offer. This was such a happy moment for her, finally getting the pay she deserved. How could he tell her that they couldn't celebrate? He wouldn't do that to her, not after he had spent the past several months working non-stop and leaving her home alone every night. How had he let his own spending get so out of hand? How could he hide this from Cynthia, how could he lie right to her face?

A solution popped into his mind. They were members at a local winery that offered them the monthly bottle of wine in the mail and once a year, dinner on the house. They hadn't made use of this perk yet, but it was an option. He dialed the winery as he raced home, requesting a table and to use his free dinner benefit. The hostess informed him that Friday evenings were the most crowded, but he insisted. She reminded him that the table may not be ideal, but that they would make room for such a loyal customer.

One problem solved. They would celebrate Cynthia's job offer, get through the two-week transition period, and start attacking the debt once she got her first new paycheck. This was it, the plan he had devised would work. If only he could have known how insignificant his plan was in the scheme of things, how he would never get a chance to make another payment on any of his debt.

Cynthia was already halfway into a bottle of white zinfandel when Timothy arrived home. She heard the soft hum of the engine and the garage door from the back patio where she was skimming through a new magazine. She had arrived home to see a cockroach in the sink. Not letting this evil creature ruin her day, she put a bright post-it note on the faucet that read "Kill Please" and headed outside to escape the insect.

It took a few moments for Timothy to join her outside, no doubt eliminating the problem that she had left for him to sort out. When she heard the sliding glass door open and close behind her she turned and smiled. She gave him the smile that had won over his heart, the one that said, "you make me the happiest woman ever." Timothy was in awe of how her hair was shining in the afternoon sun.

They say that money can't buy you happiness, but this new job, and the money it offered were certainly already helping to bridge the void that had grown between the Lawsons. Cynthia offered Timothy a glass as he told her they had a little under an hour until their table would be ready at the club. Cynthia drained the rest of her wine glass and moved to head back into the house to change her outfit.

Timothy gently grabbed her arm, stopping her, and pulled her closer for a kiss. A kiss, how long had it been since they had kissed at all, let alone like they meant it? Surely, this was the beautiful moment that would mark the beginning of the next phase of their marriage. A happier and healthier phase.

They were both so absorbed in the moment, in the magic of all that the new job and its increased salary could do, that neither of them realized that the pond was noticeably less full than it had been just a day earlier.

chapter 28

D AY 0, THE final day of the countdown and the first day before the "after" for the Ryechiks. Jack had been too excited to sleep. Melinda tossed and turned a bit, but eventually fell into a sound sleep. She could have slept until the mid-morning, but she didn't take advantage of that opportunity. She was up and awake early with Jack, packing everything and checking their list of supplies for the twelfth time.

The first step was complete, and the hardest for sure. Perhaps it was best classified as the pre-step, or steps. Their checklist to get ready was done, and now it was time to execute.

They had been preparing for years really, but the pieces had all come together in the past few months. Every item was necessary to set up their grand finale. During that time, they kept their home tidy and allowed their accomplice, Ryan Moore, unlimited access to the premises. He was in on their scheme and he loved the excitement of their plan. They decided to keep things quiet a little longer.

But, just a few weeks earlier they had received a call from Ryan, some unexpected but extremely good news. They could move up their deadline. When did things ever happen earlier than planned? How did they get so lucky? Perhaps their plan was destined to work after all. As Timothy was taking Cynthia out to a dinner they could ill afford, Jack and his wife were getting the last of their items packed to prepare for the big moment, imminent as it loomed over their horizon. The grand finale was ready to be put into place.

That day, that last day in their house on Hurley Pond was so clear to the Ryechiks. They were calm, surprisingly calm. It felt like their wedding day all over again, so much anticipation and worry over what could go wrong and then they were delightfully surprised by how much went right.

Jack took the afternoon to finish the edits to the post that would go up on their website. Of course, this was going up on their website. They had plans, a vision, no, a mission that they needed to bring to the American people. They had advice that they hoped would convert others into following their mission. And where else could Jack express his frustrations and find those who shared his thoughts? Where did he find such camaraderie and eventually the seed that would develop into the idea for this grand plan? The internet, with chat rooms and blogs to encourage his off-kilter desires and propel him to the successful execution of his scheme.

Melinda read over the post, adding her comments, toning down what she thought was necessary, leaving in the asides that could reveal their identity. They had thrived on the anonymity that the internet offered. Strangers thousands of miles away were connecting with them, commenting on their posts, encouraging them in their plan, but they were still worried about what their family would think. Melinda shrugged, they would all find out in a few hours anyway. No stopping it now.

They would all know about the details of their plan. Their family members would be asked the same questions about their strange relatives and their crazy plan after the fact. And they would find the blueprint for that plan, each detail, each step, on their website. A series of posts and articles that laid out how to execute such a plan, encouraging others and instructing them how to do the same.

Melinda smiled as she scheduled the post to go live at precisely 7:00pm. At that point, everyone would be in place, the crowd would be gathered, it would be too late to stop any of it.

With their resounding proclamation set to publish, they prepared for the video they would post on their channel at the same time. This was an important moment, and what better way to explain why they were doing what they were doing, than a video. People probably wouldn't understand, they would roll their eyes and say that the pair of them were crazy, but Jack and Melinda had heard all of that before.

They checked their looks in the mirror before they turned on the camera. "You ready?" Jack whispered as he gently touched her elbow, reassuring her of his connectedness. She didn't look at him directly, but met his gaze in the mirror. The entire bathroom was empty save for her small make-up bag that she was slowly putting her items back into.

Melinda wiped away, what he thought was a lone, errant tear. "Yep," she smiled at him so sweetly and with genuine joy. Their destiny had arrived and with it, their fate, the fate of everyone who knew them: loved ones, friends, and neighbors, was sealed.

They sat down together at the folding table in the empty room that had once contained a desk. Even though it had none of the hallmarks of one, this was their at-home office, or at least it was. In the last two chairs remaining in the house, dining table chairs with the seat cushions, they seated themselves. The chairs were in the exact spot that they had tested so that they would both be visible on camera. Jack clicked the record button on the webcam and then began his rehearsed statement. Under the table and off-screen he reached for Melinda's hand and gave it a slight squeeze.

"...Today is the day that we pull the trigger."

chapter **29**

H ER BRIGHT MOOD in light of her new job offer seemed to help Cynthia ignore the fact that their table was right next to the kitchen. Or maybe she was aware of it, but was in too good a mood to make any negative comments. Whatever the reason for the absence of her usual complaints, Timothy was glad to have a nice evening out with his wife. A celebration.

They chit-chatted as they got ready for the dinner and drove to the restaurant going over the minute details of the interview itself, the offer that was made, the potential savings by accepting the offer. After they had selected their meals, they reviewed what to say to her boss to help Cynthia leverage an agreeable counteroffer. Timothy was skeptical that she would receive a counteroffer; he didn't want to lead her to think that it was a lock, but he couldn't crush her spirits either.

Once their plates appeared they dove head first into their meals, their foreheads bobbing slightly as they ate with an unorganized cadence. There was no room for talking at this point, they were famished, and Cynthia was starting to feel the wine go to her head.

As they began to abate, slowing their chewing, taking longer breaks between each bite, they sat in silence. One chewing, the other waiting for them to finish. Back and forth they went in silence. Cynthia began to let her eyes wander around the restaurant, the lighting was always set way down and each table had real candles lit, not the fake plastic kinds, the real ones that offered real heat.

"This really is such a nice restaurant," Cynthia finally offered up.

Timothy agreed and ran with the topic that she had started. But, within a few moments even that let up. Even with all of the excitement that they had both felt an hour prior, their interest in each other was almost reduced to zero. They both wondered how they had drifted so far apart. Timothy used to tell Cynthia every detail of the cases he was working on, but he didn't even know where to start to describe the Hyrdoline case.

He knew that if they were going to really come back to each other, they would need to face the void head on. He began to build up the courage to finally ask her why they didn't talk to each other anymore. He knew that asking it would start a long conversation, perhaps a nasty one, but one that needed to happen. He took a breath in and opened his mouth to speak.

"Cynthia, -" he started hesitantly, waiting for her eyes to meet his.

"Oh, my goodness! Tim?" he heard from across the room. The tall and busty blonde that he had been flirting with earlier that afternoon was striding towards their table.

Cynthia's eyes gave her a quick once over. Her defensive and territorial instincts began to kick in. The evaluation had been mutual; Kellyanne had been eyeing the Lawson's table for some time. She knew that Timothy was married, she could see his ring, but given the many nights that he spent eating dinner with her and not his wife, she assumed that a divorce was imminent. It had to be, right?

"I didn't expect to see you here!" she continued cooing as she beamed down at them, the smile on her face was so wide and so sparkling that it was noxious, it was clearly a fake.

"Hey," was all that Tim could muster. "Funny running into you here," he was finally able to add after he took a moment to try to figure out how to wiggle his way out of the imminent questions from his wife. "This is my lovely wife Cynthia," he gestured to her with an open palm, not pointing one finger but offering his hand up as a platter, a pedestal where he could set the image of his wife.

"Oh hello," Cynthia responded as she took a sip from her wine glass, her other hand was occupying her lap, balled into a fist just below the table and out of view. She made no effort to exchange pleasantries. Inside her mind, she was running through an infinite number of scenarios in which Timothy would have cheated on her with this woman. This tall, pretty, skinny woman. Suddenly the waistband of her jeans felt like it was digging into her skin, pushing her belly upward into an unflattering roll.

Only one small speck of mental space was fighting hard to remind her that she could trust Timothy. She then reminded herself about her own flirting with Erik, and that near kiss the other day. Maybe Timothy had given in, gone further. Maybe he was weak when faced with temptation, not Cynthia. She could invite temptation in and stare it in the face and not budge. Although she might have given in if the moment hadn't been ruined; she reminded herself that she was totally innocent. She hadn't kissed another man; she hadn't done anything physical. She was innocent and Timothy was a lying cheater. She drained the rest of her glass of wine as the woman, *the other woman*, finally waved good-bye to Timothy and walked away.

It was true, she had been gaining weight, her mind went to that old insecurity first. Cynthia felt partially to blame for not keeping him interested. Was he really working all those nights that he came home late? Should she have asked him for more details, wait, had she asked about any details? When was the last time they had sex? Surely, they did last month, but maybe he was too tired. Her brain was starting to swim, her memories sloshing in the wine that she had been drinking all night.

Timothy was looking at her now, he looked guilty. He looked like a man who was hoping that his wife wouldn't make the connection between him and his lover. Maybe it was her subtle way of spilling the beans, making herself known. Perhaps for Cynthia's benefit, perhaps for her own. She was either marking her territory or she was fed up with Timothy, jilted by him, and now she wanted to expose their little secret. Either way, Cynthia was barely containing her rage.

"So, uh, what were we talking about," Timothy tried to awkwardly dive back into the conversation as he pushed a forkful of pasta into his mouth.

She just looked at him across the table. *Should she ask now? Should she make a scene at the club?* No, she would wait. She would patiently and calmly wait to have this conversation at home. Not in the car where they might get into a wreck. At home. In the privacy of their own house.

"We've gone over the new offer. It is great, but ideally, my current job will counter and we will just keep on the same path." Cynthia spoke looking down into her lap, straightening out the linen tablecloth lying across her thighs.

"Well, maybe. We could save on gas money if you took this new job."

Was he really trying to get his way, to push his agenda? After that little stunt? She took a deep breath and brushed her hair back behind her shoulders.

"Do you want to take the rest of that to go?" she asked casually, still not making eye contact. She pushed her plate away from her and folded her arms. She began to look around for the waiter, for any waiter, to come and clear her plate. *Come, servant, come now, I want to go; this isn't fun or special anymore.*

They drove home in silence. Each stop light was excruciatingly long. They were both left to the thoughts that were bouncing around, growing and proliferating, within the confines of their skulls. He had always imagined that every story that showed someone just accidentally falling into an affair was a load of crap. Because he felt that he had just fallen into an attraction that he was unable to control. But he was lying to himself. The lies he was trying to put into his own brain were unconvincing. He had taken steps along the way, he had fantasized and dreamed of her.

In grade school, the nuns taught him that a sin was when someone intentionally turned from God. He had in fact sinned against his wife, consciously turned from her with each late night at the bar, each message to and from Kellyanne, each time he failed to defend her, each time he belittled her materialistic ways. The lust for this new person had come too easily. But so had his initial lust for Cynthia.

It was effortless to lust for someone. And in time, his desire for Cynthia had turned into love. It was only logical that the next step was marriage. The Lawsons hadn't worked for it, so it seemed improbable that they would work now to speak to one another, to communicate, to save what had fallen into their laps.

In all of the ways that Timothy was chaffed about that evening, he never once swore to himself that enough was enough. He didn't make a silent vow of 'never again', he smarted over the free meal that was ruined by a chance encounter. He was so hurt that Cynthia wasn't even speaking to him, after he took her out to a nice dinner, after he rushed home to celebrate with her. *Nothing was ever good enough*, he repeated to himself.

As the car pulled along Hurley Pond, the Lawsons began to shift, to fidget. Once the car was parked and they were inside, the fight, the screaming match of the century would erupt between them. Cynthia hoped that it would end quickly with tears over nothing, a sweet touch, and some glorious make-up sex. Timothy hoped that she wouldn't scream too loud at him, preparing to be embarrassed if the neighbors found out that they were fighting. It's not like every couple doesn't fight, but the Lawsons were above being normal, they were not like everyone else. Their clothes and cars and careers should have been proof enough of that fact. They were better than the rest, even if they were following the same motions as everyone else.

Their attentions shifted to their own home as it came into view, but they were both very quickly distracted by the sight laid out before them.

Lights.

Lights as bright as daylight flooding the street.

"What the-" Timothy wondered out loud as they tried to pull into their own garage. The street was blocked, too many cars, too many bright lights taking over the Ryechik's lawn.

Cynthia's mouth slowly turned from a tight, pursed, mad-at-Timothy frown to a gaping, wide "o" of wonder and horror.

chapter **30**

THE POST THAT the Ryechik's had left on their blog, "Chekin' Out", very popular among certain circles, announced the execution of their plan. Announcing to the world that their countdown was finished, tonight was the night.

They had invited their close friends and relatives, telling them each that it would be a small intimate dinner. When asked what they could bring, they were each told to bring wine or beer. The Ryechik's had made themselves a nice little going-away party.

There wasn't enough room to park, cars were flowing out into the street, creating a narrow passage for everyone else to try and squeeze their way through. What did Jack and Melinda care? This was their last night in that neighborhood. Mrs. Schor, usually very particular about noise levels on the block, had agreed to let the guests park in her driveway as long as she could attend the party. The Ryechiks told her that her presence was not just requested, but in fact, required. The old woman beamed as she sat underneath the array of bistro lights that Jack had spent most of the day hanging. It really did look like it was the middle of the day on their lawn. Melinda offered Mrs. Schor an extra pair of sunglasses, the ones that she always picked up for free from here or there.

Even though their blog was relatively successful, bringing in a couple thousand dollars in revenue each month, the Ryechiks usually hated to make a spectacle of themselves. Maybe that's why they never mentioned it to the Lawsons in their limited conversations. But that night was special, it was different. Jack and Melinda were okay with creating a big event, putting themselves in the center of attention for just one night. It was a big one, and they were both beaming with excitement.

As everyone gathered and began to nibble at the food that was pre-pared, the din of voices grew louder. Guests drank the wine and beer collected on one of the folding tables. There were post-it notes on each folding chair stating who would be taking it home at the end of the night. Signs were put up on the food and beverage table stating that all items must go. They jokingly call it their "F.I.R.E. sale" and only a few people in the crowd got the joke and laughed heartily. The rest were confused but happy to take the free food and drink and wait patiently for an explanation.

The energy on their front lawn was palpable. Most of the guests had no idea what was going on. Surely, there was some big announcement to be made. Jack's parents and his lone aunt and uncle were speculating as they chewed on their hot dogs: maybe Melinda really was pregnant. Although that wouldn't account for their empty house. Jack's mom, Sabrina, had a feeling in her gut that something was about to take her son away from her for a long time.

Women's intuition maybe, but she felt that maybe everyone around her was too excited, too happy. That something big was about to wreck her world. She lived only ten miles from her son, an empty house could mean that they were about to move. She tried to keep up her smile and fiddled with the pendant hanging around her neck. All of the others in the crowd seemed so happy to eat free food, drink communal beers, and assume that everything was going to be just fine.

Bursts of hearty laughter erupted at odd moments. It was too loud for her, too happy. Something was about to happen; she could just feel it. She scanned the crowd for her son's face, smiling and kind. She didn't see him at the top of the driveway by the open garage, where people were milling in and out to look at some big object that Sabrina couldn't see from where she was standing. He wasn't near the food nor was he keeping the elderly woman sitting by herself company.

As she began to feel a slight pinch in her chest, she saw a pair of pale and lanky arms waving above the crowd. "Hey, everyone," could be just barely heard above the clamor of noises. A sharp wolf whistle silenced the conversations, all eyes turned to Melinda, her thumb and forefinger just exiting her mouth. Jack and Melinda stood up on two short step-stools, giving them a bit of height over the rest of the crowd. One hundred in-dividual eyeballs focused on the younger Ryechiks. *Here it is*, thought

Sabrina. As Jack clasped Melinda's hand and took a deep breath in, steeling himself for the public announcement that they were about to make, a light flashed across their faces from a set of headlights pulling into the house next door. The Ryechik's faces were illuminated for a moment, their blazing smiles were revealed.

chapter 31

THOROUGHLY DISTRACTED FROM the impending argument that waited for them just inside the confines of their home, the Lawsons parked the car and began walking over to the Ryechik's lawn. Like moths in the trance of a bug light, drawn in blindly, not even noticing how close they were getting, not even realizing that they had made the conscious decision to walk over to see what was going on. They were just there.

And just in time too. Jack was in the middle of talking. "Many of you know, or have read..." a murmur went through some of the crowd with one or two uncoordinated clappers far off. He recapped the gist of it, of the blog. The extreme saving and successful investments, the years working to hone their passions and now the big announcement. A five-year trip around the world.

"We'll miss everyone, and will be sad to miss big milestones. We aren't leaving to hurt anyone and we don't expect everyone to try to do what we are doing, but we head out tomorrow in our camper. New owners move in on Monday."

Cynthia felt her jaw drop, it swung open so easily as though the force of gravity was pulling heavier on her lower mandible than on any other part of her body. Maybe she was still a little buzzed. She couldn't have heard any of those words correctly. She looked over to Timothy who looked utterly confused. They were both thinking it. How could these two people who were so poor that they couldn't even afford a car for Melinda to be able to drive to work, be able to save enough to quit their jobs and travel the world?

"We're outta here!" Jack yelled to the crowd.

chapter 32

JACK FINISHED HIS little speech, pulling Melinda in for a quick kiss. She held him back for a moment before correcting him.

"We're 'Chekin out!'" Jack nodded and Melinda let him get that kiss that he wanted. Most of the crowd was clapping. It seemed that half of the crowd was maybe in on it, maybe knew about this beforehand. Others were raising their eyebrows still, in disbelief, already anticipating the exact number of days it would take them to run out of money.

This wasn't some new goal that they had just set at the beginning of the summer. This was the culmination of a five-year plan. This was something that they had been working towards purposefully. Jack had started his lifetime savings at the age of ten when he created an account on the newly developed eBay and started selling off the board games from the family cupboard. It took three months for his parents to notice. Once they realized, he decided to focus his efforts on selling his own belongings, like the baseball cards he never looked at anymore. Jack financed his first year at college on those funds.

The concept itself wasn't what was so repugnant to the average consumers that slog through week after week, year after year, grinding out their workdays and commutes. Everyone knows that they should save for retirement. The accepted wisdom says to save ten percent, pay yourself first, retire at the legal age that you can start to withdraw from social security. That is was most people do, they follow the common knowledge, they do what they are told. They also buy the new car because they're told it will lead them on the road to greatness, whatever that means. They also get the premium cable package, because it is only ten more dollars a month for five hundred more channels. What a deal.

No, what really frustrates most people about what Jack and Melinda did, this wild plan of theirs, is that they didn't think of it themselves. That they couldn't think their way through the simple math first. They balked at the idea that Jack and Melinda could be laughing as they counted their piles of cash, enjoying a joke at the expense of their relatives who so casually threw their money down the drain in the art of living the American Dream.

The Lawsons began to feel that irritation immediately. The same irritation that most people felt when they learned about *the plan*. Cynthia was already thinking to herself, *how selfish, they have all that money and they aren't going to donate it.* Yes, Cynthia was thinking this. The same person who drove past a homeless man every day and tried her best to ignore him. The same person who turned off the TV when a children's aid commercial popped up, irritated at the harsh reality of the world being broadcast into her home. Pure irony like that doesn't occur often in literature, but there you have it, folks. Like a neon sign flashing in bright fuchsia above Cynthia's head: IRONY.

Timothy was feeling a mix of wonder and betrayal. Weren't he and Jack becoming friends? How was this big detail of their lives not shared? All of the financial worries that he had been trying to sort through the past few weeks began to flood back into his mind. How could he be so far behind Jack? They were about the same age, had nearly identical homes, both had beautiful wives and seemed to generally be happy. How could the two be on such different paths, but be so close in so many other ways?

Dumbstruck, the Lawsons moved their eyes over the scene before them as the Ryechiks worked their way through the crowd to greet their neighbors and friends. Their evening continued to take them on a rollercoaster ride of emotions with new information unfurling at a rapid speed, with still more to come. Their neighbors now hijacked the date night that they thought was spoiled by the hint of infidelity.

Cynthia's mind was sputtering. She was now starting to question the verity of the statements just made. How could these queer little people retire already? They clearly didn't have the kind of money that the Lawsons had. As Jack and Melinda finally reached the Lawsons they called out, "Oh hello!"

The bitterness running through Cynthia's mind spilled out in response, her social manners completely abandoned as her brain reeled with information overload. "But you don't have any furniture!"

"Ah yes, we started selling it off early. We were just a little zealous about it."

"Yes, and someone sold our coffee pot forgetting that we would need that for the van." Melinda patted Jack affectionately on the arm. It seemed that she was on such a high from the excitement that the poison in Cynthia's words couldn't reach her.

"Yes, sorry if our house had a mausoleum feel to it," Jack smiled widely. He was either ignoring the confused and somewhat disgusted faces on his neighbors, or he was unable to notice their subtle sneers because of the artificial lights strewn across the lawn.

The idle chatter was slipping over Cynthia. *But, what about the Mahaskals?* For some reason, she had been so set on linking the two couples in a morbid way that she couldn't reconcile all of the information and assumptions that went along with it. *What about all of the clear signs that the Ryechiks were homegrown terrorists?* Jack's odd comments. The information on the calendar. It all had to lead to them being part of some kind of syndicate.

chapter **33**

"WE'RE LUCKY THAT they are leaving before they turn this neighborhood into a hippie commune." Timothy had barely latched the door behind him when he began his own tirade. *How could they even save enough for that? I bet that came from family money and made some dumb-luck investments; it isn't possible.* "They are subversive. And being subversive is dangerous, they threaten our whole way of life. If everyone just retired early, then the world would come to a halt. Hoarding all that money, they're not helping anyone." Surprising even himself, Timothy realized that he sounded like his father, labeling the Ryechiks as subversive. Who even used that term anymore?

Cynthia was standing quietly by the island in the kitchen, her elbows gently supporting her as she waited for Timothy to stop talking. It seemed that once they entered the house her brain switched back to the most pressing topic that needed to be addressed. *Was Timothy having an affair?* She waited for him to stop speaking, for him to notice that she wasn't responding, for him to realize that they were both now in the hallowed space that would be the stage of their argument, *the argument*, the one that needed to happen.

"Who was that woman who came up to our table tonight?" she whispered. It was the first time Timothy had heard her whisper in a silent room. Her voice sounded so much less powerful, as though it was calling to him from a thousand miles away, when really his wife was just an arm's distance from him.

"She is the waitress at the sports bar across the street from the office," Timothy offered dismissively. He knew that he had done nothing wrong, nothing that could be defined anyway. How do you characterize something as flirting if a kiss doesn't follow it? How could he scroll through the texts that they had exchanged to show his innocence when there were several smiles and winks in between the orders for burgers and chicken tenders?

"Hmm," Cynthia let her disbelief hang in the air. *You're caught. Fess up or cut it out.* That was what she wanted to convey to him, but before Cynthia could think of a quick response to really cut into Timothy, he blurted out the one thing that had been on his mind, "we're broke."

He detailed the current state of their finances and their need to cut back. He was more precise this time, not sparing her any details. Another wallop to Cynthia's overstimulated psyche. *The job offer. Timothy potentially having an affair. The neighbors are secretly rich and moving out. We're broke.* She began to shake her head, an involuntary reflex to see if she could make this reality go away.

"Yes, please listen, Cynthia. I can't do this without you. We need to stick to a plan," he moved closer to her, coming around the island so that he could stand next to her. So that he could touch her arm, soothe her as he delivered the grim news. It was a form of persuasion, the subtle and soft contact of his fingertips on her skin. It was his only weapon against her stubborn mind, his ability to sway her to see reason.

I can't do this without you. The words replayed in Cynthia's mind, the rest of the trouble starting to recede from her focus.

I can't do this without you. Then he wasn't cheating, he wouldn't cheat on her. He wouldn't have an affair. He needed her. The sentiment that had been absent from their discussions since they were engaged was now back. She could take this on with him. She turned her head to look at him, refocusing on what he was saying.

"I've printed out all of our statements. I was so excited about your news that I left them at the office. I figured we could celebrate this weekend and then get down to business on Monday."

"Okay," she uttered. A quiet acquiescence that, once offered, immediately alleviated the strain on Timothy.

"Okay? Okay!" he realized that he shouldn't have been so excited, given the topic. This was day 0 of a long journey they would need to take, to get their debt to a *reasonable* level. He would need to look up what an acceptable range was for the average American household. He didn't even want to start thinking about paying it all off. That was impossible. How could anyone in America live without debt? As if on cue, a roar of laughter spilling over from the Ryechiks infiltrated the walls of their house. *Oh, well they're just crazy.* His mental reassurances were flimsy, he even began to wonder what he had done so wrong and they had done so right to be able to retire in their young thirties.

"So, what do we do now?" Cynthia looked up at him, her deep eyes beckoning his affections. Timothy started to outline the worst of their debt: their credit cards that needed to be addressed. He mentioned specific ones that they would need to stop using immediately. The ones with the highest interest had to be paid off and eliminated.

"We also need to look at all of our subscriptions. Some of these items that are ten dollars a month here and five dollars a month there are adding up. We can cancel them now and add them back on once the debt is taken care of." He saw the look of panic on Cynthia's face.

"But Bentley loves his toy delivery!" she protested.

"There are several that we can choose from, the ones that we use the least, okay?" Again, the reassuring touch on her arm. "We'll go through each of them tomorrow and decide on a few that each of us can live without until this is resolved."

Cynthia nodded. She was trying to process it all, trying to take it all in slowly and calmly. She noticed something dark in her peripheral vision. *Wretched roach.* She jumped back, terrified, only to realize that she had been alarmed by Timothy's keys sitting on the counter.

"What is it?" Timothy asked at the first sign of her distress.

"It's nothing," she covered her face with her palm. "I just thought I saw *one*," she let the rest of the meaning pass through to Timothy. That's right, another bad night. They both knew that the sleeping pills only made the nightmares worse.

"It's okay. I'll be there to protect you," Timothy so quickly slipped back into the role of the loving husband. He would be there to protect Cynthia from all of the real and imagined troubles that were plaguing them.

"Thank you, baby," she reached out to him for a hug. They shared a sweet moment. One that could have remained sweet, the two of them falling into each other, quickly forgiving all betrayals. But then Timothy had to open his mouth.

"Don't worry honey. I'll protect you from the little bad guys and the *big* bad guys," he emphasized the words, deepening his voice to show just how big and bad these amorphous evils could be.

"Like the terrorists next door," Cynthia joked. Timothy laughed a little at that one.

"More like the people trying to steal our identity," Timothy admitted in one breath.

"What!?" Cynthia was shocked and quickly pulled away to face Timothy, her perfectly trimmed eyebrows begging to know more.

"Yeah, I didn't want to bring that up too with everything else, but it looks like someone took out a loan in your name."

Was it the truth, the shock of realizing that a crime had been perpetrated, which caused Cynthia's face to respond in that manner? He saw her eyebrows reach upward, perhaps the realization that they had both been to careless, happy to assume that the money would just take care of itself was dawning on her.

"What kind of loan?" The words were so soft that they sound waves barely resonated in his eardrums.

"It doesn't say, but it is showing up in your name. I'm so sorry honey," he tried to console her. The identity theft was committed against her after all; she was now a victim of a crime. She hung her head and let her long hair fall so that it covered her face in one slow and smooth motion.

He knew that look. She had done the same thing when he found out that she had sold his older game consoles to fund a new entertainment system, all without his knowledge. She had done the same thing when he asked her about what specific jewelry she had been wanting for a birthday, only to find out that she had purchased it for herself already. That was her guilty look.

Timothy sighed audibly, for effect. It was the only response he could offer. "Is it something that we shouldn't contest?" Cynthia shook her head once, slowly.

All of that good will and positive energy that had been building vanished; it was smoke that was whisked away by the central air fans.

Timothy set his jaw and walked away, out of the kitchen, up the stairs, and into the dark hallway. She heard the guest room door close behind him. The conversation was over; there was nothing left to say before they could both process the reality that they were in, that they had finally woken up into. It seemed that once this secret crawled out of the woodwork, it was truly one that infested their home. Nothing could make it clean again, nothing could rid them of this pestilence.

She wanted to explain and make it clear that she was completely justified. Cynthia had repeated all of her reasons to herself hundreds of times over the past year and a half as she signed for and made the monthly payments. But she was too tired to even speak, although her mind was racing. How could she let this happen, how could she have been so careless to let him find out? The panic and the fear were starting to hit her, but so was another emotion. Relief. Like a piece of paper that longs to be burned, this secret of Cynthia's needed to be released, to be exposed for how big and uncontrollable it had become.

The situation that both Cynthia and Timothy created for themselves was all too common. Following any current movies or TV shows or books, you would expect it to be their infidelity. But, no, that is far less common than you would think based on popular media. Every movie has a cheater; every book has a two-timer. But that isn't so in the real world. What is so blatantly common about them is their overwhelming debt fueled by their rampant desire to spend themselves into a higher tax bracket. They longed to be special, set apart. And they were set apart, but in the worst way possible. A faithless marriage on a foundation of lies.

Yes, that was a not-so-subtle foreshadowing. I've told you all along, the Lawsons are about to meet their end.

chapter 34

TIMOTHY WOKE WITH a start and then a quick piercing pain. The start, he didn't recognize the ceiling that he opened his eyes to, the ceiling of their guest room, still undecorated and unorganized. The piercing pain, his neck lolled into a sharp angle sometime after he finally fell asleep. The jolt of panic when he didn't recognize the room, even for a fraction of a second, caused his head to jerk, forcing his neck muscles to spasm.

As his hand tried to sooth the muscles, still massaging even after the pain subsided, he recalled the previous evening. Cynthia never tried to knock on the door to explain herself. She never denied anything, never asked him to come to bed. He did hear her scream out once, faint and through the door. Probably just another nightmare.

How had their evening broken down so quickly? An afternoon of great news and celebration soon turned into one of betrayal. Cynthia taking out that loan was unconscionable. Then he recalled Kellyanne coming up to their table at dinner. An eye for an eye maybe. But he hadn't cheated, not technically, not really. So, it wasn't an even score. He didn't even know what time it was, but the sun was coming through the cheap blinds that Cynthia had on her list of things to replace.

For a brief instant, he wondered if he had dreamed the whole thing, the party next door and their neighbors' bizarre plan. But he was still in the guest room, so potentially not a dream at all. He heard a slight whimper at the door. Bentley needed to go outside to do his business. Usually, Cynthia would have him curled up in bed with her, maybe she locked him out of the room the night before. Maybe she hadn't even slept there, he might have totally imagined her screams during the night.

On his feet before he could remind himself that she had betrayed him, he opened the door and crossed the hall to find the master bedroom doors open and the bed empty. The sheets were nicely tucked in and the duvet folded the way that Cynthia liked it. Maybe she hadn't slept there the night before, or she had simply made the bed that morning. He swung his focus to the clock on his nightstand. 6:45 am.

There was no way that she was up at this hour, Cynthia always preferred to sleep in on Saturdays. As Timothy tried to reconcile the conflicting information in his brain, Bentley whimpered again and pawed at his ankle. Scooping the dog up in his arms, Timothy carried him downstairs, head on-swivel, scanning for signs of his wife.

Everything in the kitchen was put away and clean, the back door to the patio was closed and locked, the curtains were drawn. The front room was empty too. As he peered out of the blinds, Bentley whimpered again, his eyes pleading for relief. Timothy opened up the front door and set the dog down, he jumped free from his owner's arms and squatted on the first patch of grass off of the entry way.

Timothy kept an eye on Bentley, making sure a squirrel wasn't about to lure him across the yard and into the path of a car. It was only a moment later when Bentley bounced back towards the front door that Timothy dropped his gaze to the item sitting on the front porch.

Wrapped in a red satin bow was a bouquet of sorts: a hammer with a wooden handle, a flathead screwdriver with a green and white plastic grip, a rusted wrench, and a black crowbar with chipped lacquer. Timothy picked up the items and read the note tied onto the bow, "Didn't get a chance to hand these to you last night. Best of luck with all the home repairs and projects. If you can't do it with these four tools, it probably doesn't need fixing. Best of luck- Jack"

Timothy glanced to his right; the driveway was empty. The front lawn looked a little worn but otherwise clean. They were really gone. As he began to think on how much the Ryechiks had already accomplished and the stark comparison to Timothy and the financial situation he was in, Cynthia rounded the curb. Sporting her rarely used workout clothes, she was power walking with a water bottle in hand.

She walked up the drive with her eyes down, ashamed. Her contrition was a pulsing energy that she was trying to push towards Timothy with every molecule in her body. After he had walked away the previous evening, the first thought in her mind was, *maybe this was a lie he would leave me over*. She spent the entire evening cleaning, unable to sleep. She got dressed around 6:00 am when the sun came up and went for a long walk. When she saw the Ryechik's van pull away, she darted behind a tree so that they wouldn't see her.

When she got back to the house and saw Timothy, she didn't offer any explanation or demand any. She didn't want to fight so she made breakfast. Afterwards, she announced that she would need a new outfit to wear on Monday when she put in her notice at work. Timothy wanted to object, but didn't. Had she not listened to his warnings about their financial situation? But either she was starting a job with a higher salary or she would get a counter offer from her current job. More money was going to be coming in. He responded with a simple, "okay, have fun."

And that's how the entire weekend went, silent, complicit, unquestioning. Timothy continued to sleep in the guest room, not ready to forgive her for lying to him, for taking out money to pay for such frivolous items. Cynthia didn't want to face up to it, and she didn't want to start crying. She knew it would only push him further into the arms of this other woman. She wanted to ask the question directly, are you cheating? She knew deep down that he wasn't, but what if she was wrong. The truth would hurt either way. Either he was cheating and she would be crushed, or he was being faithful and she would be the lone traitor in their marriage.

Silence.

Timothy tinkered about in the garage, rearranging things, moving heavy items. He felt accomplished in this task; he relished his ability to hide away in the concrete cave of their three-car garage. When Cynthia returned, she parked in the driveway and went through the front door. They were able to slip past each other in the house without much interaction.

Silence.

That was their answer to this rift, silence until they couldn't stand it anymore. They were both secretly hoping that Monday would go in Cynthia's favor and she would get the counter offer and they could celebrate and forget that weekend ever happened.

Silence.

Silence.

That house was so quiet you could almost hear the pressure on the joists and bowing out of the drywall.

Now, at this point, you may find yourself wondering, well if the Ryechiks have moved out, then… Well…, wait? Then just who was it that blew up the Lawson's home?

PART 5

Pride

"What is our fascination with the Lawsons and their tragic story?" The moderator prompted the panel.

"Because they were a sweet young couple, living the American Dream," a respected and for-the-most-part reputable morning show host said with an air of humbled sadness to his voice.

"Were they really living the dream?" The wild card on the panel spoke up, about to offer his unpopular opinion that was already gaining him notoriety in some circles.

"What do you mean?" The moderator asked for further explanation.

The morning show host was in no mood to deal with the same rhetorical arguments that he had heard and been accused of many times. "Are we giving them too much attention because they were a white middle-class couple?"

"I wasn't going to go there, but you did. No, I meant, what is the American Dream? To buy a house so big you'll be up to your eyeballs in debt for the rest of your life, unable to do anything without that burden having to be accommodated?"

"Is that a planned diatribe or do you really think that about the Lawsons? Have some respect, they were murdered in their own home."

"That home was already their coffin. They would have had to work until the end of their natural lives to pay off everything they owed. And no, I didn't rehearse my comments. I think that about anyone who leverages their freedom against the glitter created by the best minds in advertising."

The conversation only devolved further from there, the moderator never regained control.

chapter 35

UNABLE TO SLEEP that weekend, Cynthia found that she was awake in the early hours of Monday morning. Her mind was running through the dozens of lies she told every day to her husband to cover up for the one big lie. Timothy continued to sleep in the guest room on the couch that was surely hurting his back. When she had tried to fall asleep, she quickly found herself in the same nightmare: alone, in the dark, critters crawling all over her. She sipped on colas throughout the nights by the bay window of the bedroom and read whatever books or magazines she could find. She kept the bedroom TV on, the volume off so that she could focus on the images and keep herself from slipping back into the terrifying dream.

She jerked awake at 4:30 am that morning and quickly noted that Bentley was not cuddled right up next to her. In a panic, she began to search for him. Not on the bed, not under the bed, not at the foot of the bed. She checked the master bath and finally, once she saw that the bedroom doors were cracked open, she slipped downstairs. Not on the doggie bed, not on the couch, not under the couch, not by his bowl. She began to feel that high intensity worry that she had been fighting all weekend. Her husband wasn't speaking to her, her biggest secret was exposed and threatened her marriage, and now her dog was missing. As the first molecules of fear began to set in, she noticed that the door to the patio was also ajar. *Thanks for leaving the door open all night Timothy*, she wanted to shout. *Wasn't he the one who was so worried about safety and finances? Wouldn't this little mess up potentially cost them their precious dog and an exorbitant amount of money letting the air conditioning leak outside all night?* She marched outside and began to look for Bentley. Not on the patio chair cushions, not by the outdoor water bowl, not by the grill.

She heard a sharp yipping nearby, her head moved towards the sound. Standing in the middle of a wide and shallow mud bowl where Hurley Pond had once glistened in the early morning light, Bentley was barking at the air. She ran out to get him. In one simple motion, she scooped him up and dashed back into the house, locking the door tightly behind her. She tiptoed into the mudroom and washed the gunk off her feet and legs. *What happened to the pond out there?* She only paused to think on this for a moment, rationalizing that there must not be enough rain yet that season.

She wiped her feet off on one of the towels in the top closet and then rubbed the mud off Bentley's heels. She was wide awake now and unable to fall back asleep. The hours passed slowly but, they did finally pass. She dressed for the day and rehearsed in her mind what she would say to her boss. She crept down the hallway past the closed door of the guest room. Timothy wouldn't be up for another hour, but Cynthia was eager to get out of the house. She hated the silence, and the waiting. Waiting to tell her boss that she would need to be promoted if the company wanted to keep her. Waiting for Timothy to speak to her, to acknowledge her as a person, his wife, and finally have the argument that was overdue. The waiting was the worst. She didn't want to wait any longer.

She was able to find a space on the lower floor of the parking garage, something she had never experienced before. She walked down to the corner shop for a fresh bagel and coffee that she enjoyed while the rest of the world seemed to filter into the city. The anonymity of being another professional woman in the coffee shop made her feel safe, it calmed her brain for the first time since that previous Friday evening when every-thing had started to fall apart. To the people passing by, she wasn't a liar or even a vapid consumer. She could be anybody. She could be whoever she wanted to be.

Another morning waking up in the guest room, another tight pain in his neck. Timothy stumbled from the guest room to the master bedroom, his feet heavy and tired. It took him a few minutes to realize that Cynthia was even gone; they had been so artful in evading each other all weekend that it started to seem natural that she wasn't in the bedroom when he walked in. As though she could somehow intuit the exact time to leave so that she could avoid him. This thought made him feel sad. He didn't want this kind of marriage. *He didn't want*, he paused his own thought because he knew it would be a betrayal to his cousin, *but he didn't want to end up divorced and alone like Henri*. He didn't want his life to become a train wreck, more than it already felt like.

He dressed, drove to work, and continued his morning as though nothing had happened over the weekend. Nothing out of the ordinary, nothing that was about to end his life and that of his wife's.

He tried to focus on the Hydroline case, opposing counsel had requested another postponement. Timothy would usually have already handled this when the notice came in the previous week. However, he had been distracted. The potential of Cynthia's job offer, the constant calls from the bank, the playful texts from Kellyanne. It was all too much.

After an hour of staring at the same page without processing any of the words on it, he decided to revisit the item weighing on him the most, how to get out of the financial hole they had dug themselves into. He took part of the blame, but now that he knew the truth about Cynthia's personal loan, he was able to update the columns of what they owed and how they could pay it all each month. He input the balance into the excel document he had started, the red number at the bottom of the column grew, and it appeared bolder and brighter than before. It was as if this little box on the spreadsheet was somehow mocking him.

The numbers weren't going to work until Cynthia either accepted the new job offer or got a raise at her current job. If she got the raise, he was going to insist on the two of them carpooling until they got their feet under them. He wouldn't take no for an answer, Cynthia had been lying to him about that extra loan, she owed him this much.

Within his own mind, he tried to test himself to see if he was being irrational. *Shouldn't they be able to have all the things that they want as a couple? Didn't they scrimp enough when he was in law school?* (A rhetorical question that he knew was comical because they hadn't actually cut back on anything during that time.) He continued with his line of thinking.

Wasn't it *just* money, wasn't it just a number. It wouldn't determine their happiness, right? But it could never be *just* money to them, to him. It should have made him feel more relaxed, freer, more able to make decisions without worry. But every thought he had was circumnavigating that money, its nominal value and what that would mean for his day-to-day life. To *their* day-to-day life, he had to correct himself.

Needing to accomplish some sort of task, Timothy did a cursory review of their accounts: his 401k balance, the homeowner's policy, the life insurance policies. A dark thought passed through his mind and he could hardly believe that he would even think that for a fraction of a second. He brushed that thought away, he figured that good news from Cynthia was due any minute. With her new income, things would start to work. They would just start to work, like a machine, it all had to work.

chapter **36**

HENRIETTA ARRIVED BACK to the office after lunch. She hadn't seen much of her cousin all day, although she could tell that he was there because of the dark shadow that occasionally moved behind the tinted glass of his office door. She wanted to tell him the good news that she had maybe, potentially, hopefully, found a new guy. It was premature, of course, but she wanted to tell someone. As a recent divorcee with a drinking problem and a DUI to show for it, she had used up a lot of the empathetic capital of her own friends. Henri knew that she could count on Timothy to be positive and share in her small, not-really-a-victory, but pseudo-triumph.

She softly tapped on the door to his office. A mumbled grunt on the other side was all that she could hear. She pushed the door open just a crack and peeked through. Timothy was bent over his desk, his head in his hands as he tried to force the words in front of his face to magically download into his brain. This was the most stressed she had seen him since they had been studying for the bar exam at the same time.

"Whoa, major Hydroline work today?" She was being asked to help with the case, which meant big bucks for all of the Lawsons if the ruling went in their favor.

"Yeah, a lot to read through," Timothy didn't move his head much as he spoke. He appeared to be shell-shocked. Henri knew that he took his job seriously, but she had never seen him this distraught over a case. She knew that there had to be more going on, but she didn't want to push the issue.

"Well, take a break for lunch and come back to it with fresh eyes," she offered the first bit of advice that popped into her head.

"What?" Timothy popped up in his chair.

"Just take some lunch, you need a break."

"Lunch? What time is it?" Panicked, Timothy scrambled to find his phone underneath the mountain of papers.

Dramatically lifting her wrist to read out the time of her oversized rose-gold watch, Henri announced, "1:35."

"What!?" Timothy was thumbing the screen of his smart phone.

"Is everything okay?" she finally asked, sensing her cousin's urgency.

"No, I haven't heard a thing from Cynthia today," his explanation didn't help Henri connect the dots.

"Isn't that normal though?" The words slipped out before she could rephrase them in a nicer way. She didn't get the impression that her cousin and his wife were particularly chatty with one another during the work day.

"Yes, but she got a job offer on Friday," he began to explain. "She was supposed to talk with her boss this morning to put in her notice."

"Oh, well congratulations!" This was the perfect time to slip in her little bit of good news too.

"No, I should have heard from her by now."

Henri was shut down. She didn't know how to express what was rolling through her mind. Here was her cousin, practically her brother they were so close, ignoring her for his high maintenance wife. Henri, once again, upstaged by Cynthia, regretted even knocking on his door.

"Something isn't right. She hasn't sent anything. Not even a 'wish me luck' or a 'well that's done now.' Nothing."

Henri wanted to tell him to snap out of it. Who was he imagining was his wife? The woman didn't even text him to say good luck when he went to court anymore, a habit that had dissipated in the height of the wedding planning madness that had never been reinstituted, like much of their relationship. She wanted to provide a sarcastic and snarky answer, but then she would feel awful if Cynthia really was in trouble. She stood there in limbo, not sure of what to say as Timothy picked up his car keys and excused himself.

She turned to watch him walk out through the lobby and head for the elevator. "By the way, I think I might have met someone," she whispered quietly. Alone in the office, she realized that she had no one who would worry about not receiving a message from her, no one that would rush to check on her if they sensed that something might be wrong. It was a scary and painful thought. She envied the woman that she normally couldn't stand because from the outside, it seemed nice that Cynthia got to have the house and the cars and the husband. Henri let a few tears fall quickly and then she felt the dry tug at the back of her throat, the familiar craving for a glass of chilled white wine.

chapter **37**

WHEN TIMOTHY ARRIVED home, he discovered Cynthia prostrate on the couch, a bag of candies in one hand and chips in the other. Two empty wine bottles stood on the coffee table, evidence of her mid-day binge. "Cynthia!" Timothy called out. He was surprised by how much he was worried about her as he had rushed home, how the instinct for caring about her had kicked in, even after she had lied about something so big, he still loved her. But this new sight was grotesque. Chocolate stained the edges of her teeth, brown smears across her professionally whitened pearls. Her hair was ratty, as though she had been fumbling around in an alleyway. Before he could begin to ask the many questions that were starting to fill his mind, she spoke.

Ever so simply, her lips barely moving, her voice barely breaking, "oh no dinner with your new girlfriend tonight?" It was a clear shot, a direct hit, first blood drawn.

"What? What are you talking about? I don't have a girlfriend. What in the world are you doing?" He rattled off. "And, what about your meeting? Did you put in your notice?"

Cynthia sniffled, she dropped the bags of food and quickly covered her face with her hands, the first creases of a frown beginning to cover her face. The room was dark so Timothy moved to open up the blinds. Putting aside his anger, once again, he sat next to his wife and tried to touch her, but she flinched, brushing him off.

"You've got to tell me what is going on." He tried to modulate his tone as best as he could, but he wasn't sure who he was even dealing with anymore. She had seemed less and less of Cynthia recently and more of this monster that she was turning into: a liar, a drunk, not anyone he was in love with.

"Apparently," she started with a deep sigh, "it is just delightful that I was able to find an offer and the company would like to reward me for my years of service by letting me take my two weeks' notice and spend it at home." At this, she began to cry. Her small tears hidden from view until they worked their way past her wrists and down her arms.

"What? That's actually nice." Timothy had been able to move his hand against her back, gently rubbing his fingertips up and down her spine.

"Don't you see!" Her shrill voice caused Bentley to jump. "That means that they were going to fire me! Me! They asked me to clear out my desk by lunch! I've worked so hard for that company! How could they?"

"Well, maybe that is their new policy when people give their notice," he tried to find a reasonable explanation, but what she had relayed wasn't hard to imagine either.

"No, it's not!" She snapped and shrugged his hand off her shoulder. "It was embarrassing. I hadn't told anyone else about the offer so it looked like I had been fired. They made me clean everything out in front of everyone; I didn't want to stay until lunch and watch them pity me or gossip about me."

Now her tears were visible, hot against her cheeks, cool as they pooled at the droop of her chin. "I didn't get to celebrate this new opportunity with the girls," even as she said this, she knew that it sounded juvenile and that it exposed her insecurities. But she said it anyways. "I didn't get to say goodbye to-" she stopped short. She was going to say that she didn't get to say goodbye to Erik, their chance at a final conversation, a hug maybe, cut short. But she caught herself. "-To anyone," she tried to gesticulate to show the extreme nature of the wrong that had been done to her.

She had been balancing in her mind the weight of her mistakes while she had been laying in the dark, before Timothy had arrived. What was more a betrayal, her easily identifiable flirting with Erik or the daily lie she told to Timothy about where her money, their money, went? It wasn't just the extra little shopping sprees online that she carefully hid by having the items sent to her office, but it was the monthly payments on the personal loan that she took out to cover the difference on the must-have elements of her dream wedding. It wasn't a small lie. She had to own that it was a B I G one, a $20,000 lie. No, a $20,000 plus interest lie.

She had lied then, before the wedding when she told Timothy that those extravagant lighting displays were within the budget. They certainly became more affordable once the check cleared. But every month that she feverishly checked the mail for the bill and sent off another check to pay down the principal and interest she felt more and more rotten. She was a cheating wife even if she never touched another man. She let Erik think he stood a chance, she let Timothy think she was being his model wife. She was a fake; she was the reason that she felt that her marriage was a sham.

Seeing her exposed like that made Timothy feel for her. He would forgive her, he knew it. They were in this together and he needed to comfort her. He moved towards her so that he could wrap her in a hug.

"No," she pushed him away. "You stay away from me! This was all your idea. You always resented that I never made enough money and kept pushing me to get another offer!"

Timothy was stunned speechless. *Hadn't he been supportive and encouraging? Why was all this anger being directed at him?*

"Look what you've done!" she yelled before she ran up the stairs and slammed the bedroom door. Another fight, another round of loud sobs, another night on the futon in the guest room.

chapter **38**

TIMOTHY CONTINUED HIS workweek with some semblance of normality. He was getting used to sleeping in the guest room, but the cramped futon was not going to work for him any longer. Cynthia was sleeping in well past when he left for work. When he arrived home on Tuesday, there were three new empty bottles of wine on the coffee table. He expected that she would be sleeping those off for a while. He left a note on the kitchen counter, next to her empty wine glass.

When she finally did rise, she stumbled down to the kitchen and grabbed a pudding cup from the refrigerator for breakfast. She read his note and started to feel her heart race, she felt that panic once again, one that she wanted to wash away with more wine.

Instead of opening another bottle, she went upstairs to shower and put on her jeans and a white blouse. She told herself that she needed to look the part if she was ever going to be seen as a good wife again. Especially where her husband was concerned. She gathered some supplies from the garage and then tramped back up to the guest room, not entirely sure of what to do, but certain that she had to do something.

After an hour or so, Cynthia finally gave into the heat, frustrated and directly very mad at the air conditioning that was broken, mad at her sweat, uncontrollable as it was, for besmirching her silk blouse. She shed her silk and placed it gently in a loose pile in the hallway, her dog quickly using it as a cushion for a nap, bound to snag the fabric.

She painted in her bra and underwear, finally letting herself accept that no one would ever know about her short jaunt as a chubby married lady, sweating in her underwear and painting the walls of her guest room. More importantly, she convinced herself that no one would find out why.

That her husband had a crick in his neck from his exile of sleeping on the couch and demanded that the guestroom be set up. He offered her the ultimate threat: if the guest room wasn't set up by the time he got home, he would leave.

This was all the motivation that she needed. Whether he knew about the air conditioning not working was a mystery to her, but it seemed to have only stopped working within the past hour. She got to work and kept painting, even as her hair, expensive and tailored as it was, became splattered with bits of paint. Cynthia's efforts to paint the room were admirable. Her cheater's guilt was compelling her to do this kindness for her husband. To finish this task and perhaps cross the first bridge needed to put her financial frauds behind her. No matter whether she had selected taupe, or periwinkle, or burnt Sienna for the paint, the house would still collapse and the explosion would still incinerate the drywall and all of the structural bits into an unrecognizable gray crumble.

Cynthia resolved to text Timothy once the guest room was painted so that he would know that she was working on getting the room set up. Only then, she would ask about getting someone out to service the air conditioner.

The walls were done. She took a quick photo to send to Timothy. "Paint is done. AC is broken, can you call for a repair? Will move in bed frame set once the paint is dry. Will need help with the mattress."

She didn't hear anything back from him all day. The paint finally dried so she was able to bring up the large boxes and slats that had been sitting in the garage. *Thank goodness for IKEA*, she thought as she lugged the smaller items up the stairs.

She rested after she brought the last of the items into the guest room. At the height of their solipsistic tendencies, the Lawsons had neglected their friendships to the point that genuine people started to fall back in favor of pursuing more worthwhile relationships. That left the social leeches to remain sucking at the image of glamor and upper-middle-class ascension that Timothy and Cynthia masterfully crafted. No one would ever come to visit them, no one would stay in this guest room except for Timothy. At this realization, Cynthia shrugged and headed downstairs to finally open that bottle of wine. If Timothy didn't like the guest room, he would need to either set up the bed frame himself or start acting like a man and sleep with her in the same bed again. She was going through a time now and she didn't want to continue to be punished for a mistake she had made years earlier.

In the afternoon, as she polished off a second bottle of wine and a pint of ice cream, she heard sharp brakes just outside the house. Expecting the AC repairman to be coming by, although Timothy had made no response yet, she just assumed he had made the call, she popped over to the door to peek through the blinds.

The busy movements and accompanying sounds of workers arriving at, what had been the Ryechik's home, initially disappointed her, but otherwise didn't really interest Cynthia. She didn't want to restart the mating ritual whereby new neighbors introduce and size one another up. She felt that she would certainly fail. She returned to her couch and her chardonnay.

As the day-time television shows progressively began to grow more and more repetitive, she sauntered to the front room, the same boxes still stacked in the corner, the same swatches of paint on the wall, to peer out at the new neighbors through the blinds.

She saw a polished young couple. They looked positively chic. Their hair had the perfect sheen, her boots the right shade of light brown, his watch glinting in the mid-day sunlight. The pair were conducting an orchestra of men with forms and plans. The vans parked outside spelled out exactly what they were up to: a complete remodel. Tiling, flooring, painting, landscaping. All scheduled to meet for a consultation on the same day, allowing them to detail how they could work together. *Smooth*, Cynthia admitted with a hint of smug jealousy pushing up her left eyebrow and forcing her lips to purse.

Downtown, a very different type of assessment was being made. Timothy was trying to get a full grasp of what he was dealing with. Unable to come to a decision in all the time he had spent alone at his desk, the answer popped into his head when his cousin walked by the door to his office, about to leave for the day.

"Henri?" Timothy's voice was almost so low that it was a whisper.

"Yes?" She stopped in the doorway of his office, but the look on his face beckoned her to step forward again, and close the door behind her. She worried that this would be another comment about Cynthia not wanting her to come around anymore. The woman had practically barred her from Timothy's life, her own cousin. It was such an overreaction to her one slip up, but as she seethed, she realized that it was the latest of many small errors and let her pride go.

"I may need the phone number for the, uh-" he paused and shook his head in disbelief of the words he was about to say. "The guy you hired…" he let the words just sit in the space between them, loaded with enough meaning to make his intent clear, or at least he thought it was clear. It was obvious to him that it was the only solution, even if he couldn't believe that it was his reality.

"I thought you had already reached out to the P.I.?" Henri had in fact hired quite a few when she first suspected her ex-husband of cheating. She had it confirmed from three independent sources, it may seem as though she was being thorough, but it had become a compulsion. She had to know more details, she had to know everything about who he was cheating with so that she could dissect the reasoning. *Ah, he's sleeping with a brunette, maybe he doesn't like my blonde hair after all.* She poured over the documents and found that she would actually get excited when she would see a call from the detectives. It was sick, she should have dreaded every moment of it. She had only stopped herself when she realized that he was probably catching on. Timothy had inquired about one of the private investigators around the 4th of July when he was almost certain that Cynthia was stepping out on him. Henrietta wasn't surprised, but she was discreet. She had never asked Timothy about whether the investigator had found anything or if he had even reached out. She guessed that she was about to find out.

"No, uh, yeah, I did. He didn't find anything." Henrietta was ashamed at her disappointment. Timothy continued, "But, I still think I may need to talk to the, uh, lawyer. That you worked with." Timothy had been looking down at his hands the entire time.

She knew what he meant and even though she should have consoled him or offered the number for a marriage counselor instead, she stood up, walked into her office, found the business card, and left it sitting right in front of Timothy. She closed his office door quietly and returned to her own office and began to cry a little. *Why did it have to be this way? Why did marriages have to end? Why did people have to be so cruel and ugly? And why, of all things, was she one of those divorced people?*

When Henri was later questioned by investigators about the relationship that Timothy had with his wife, she elected to relay his intense worry about her the day she hadn't reached out to him about her job offer. She wanted that to be how others remembered him, as a caring man. When pressed for details, she finally admitted that she gave him the information for the P.I. that had been hired, but she volunteered nothing about the business card for the divorce attorney. That evidence had gone up in smoke.

chapter **39**

BY THURSDAY, TIMOTHY was through with Cynthia's theatrics. He had enough of the silence and the tiptoeing around, waiting for her to be sober enough to talk about what was happening and what they needed to do. With each passing day, he grew more agitated and nervous about the bills that would need to be paid in short order and how they would balance them all. And each evening she was more completely and entirely inebriated than the previous.

He confronted her about her mood and told her to snap out of it and make herself useful. He wanted to grab her by her shoulders and shake her, but he didn't do that. It seemed an overdramatic gesture, one from a campy film from the 50s when women were all one moment away from hysteria. He jutted out his chin as a means of releasing his frustration, his fist planted firmly on the cold marble of the kitchen counter.

"What have you been doing all week? Have you even accepted the job offer from the plant?" Timothy demanded an answer.

Her bottom lip quivering, the skin twitching in a manner that Cynthia could not control. She hated the sensation of that motion, that shaking that she could do nothing to stop until she bit down on her lip. Timothy must have found it laughable, something else wrong with her. Tears appeared in her eyes quickly, she had been trying to keep them in, but they had appeared as if they had just been there all along, waiting for that moment.

"That job is beneath me," she tried to maintain her dignity as she spoke those hateful works. "I won't be going to work there."

The argument escalated. Timothy demanded that she call and accept the offer immediately before it was too late. She refused, stamping her foot on the ground. He screamed and asked how she couldn't see what dire financial straits they were in. How many times did he need to explain it? But she would never accept that they were in a bind. Their house was too beautiful, their clothes were too nice, and their cars were too luxurious for them to be broke. Cynthia couldn't see past the façade that they had built and Timothy had no further words to describe it to her.

She stormed upstairs to the master bedroom, heaving loud theatrical sobs that he could hear from the downstairs.

Timothy didn't want this marriage, one where they fought all the time. One where his wife never listened to him, where he was always the bad guy for trying to get them to stick to a budget. He wasn't beating her, he wasn't cheating on her, although he did have to admit that he was sore on Kellyanne coming up to them at the restaurant and making it seem as though they were. Timothy didn't want to be the guy that got divorced either.

He felt nauseated just having the business card for a divorce lawyer in his pocket. He started to wash away his unease with a beer, then another.

After a few hours, Cynthia's cries had died down, having worked herself into an exhausted slumber. Bored, and half drunk, Timothy set his cell phone alarm for work the next day.

He stepped into the kitchen and put the beer bottles in the recycling, the glass making a distinct clinking sound as they landed at the bottom of the can.

Then he went over to the oven and pulled it out from the wall, making sure that the gas hose disconnected. He could smell the faint hint of the fumes as they first wafted up to his nostrils.

He climbed the carpeted stairs mutely, without making a sound. He sat down on the newly set-up guest bed and closed his eyes.

chapter **40**

TIMOTHY WOKE UP to the sound of his phone alarm and dressed quickly, he forgot about what he had done the night before, but only for a moment. Then it came flooding back into his mind. He descended the stairs and saw a note on the counter from Cynthia.

"Sorry about yesterday, I'm struggling to be the wife that you deserve and I'm going to try better starting right now. Out for a run, let's eat breakfast together when I get back." Before he could process her words and reconcile them with his actions, before he could figure out how to re-plug the oven hose and clear out the gas, the front door opened and Cynthia came hopping in.

"That run was pretty fun. It'll be better when those kids are back in school, but for now, this is a good start. Ready for some breakfast? I'm starving!" Her post-run adrenaline high had Cynthia all hopped up, her energy was through the roof for someone who had just been on a weeklong wine-bender.

Before he could respond to her, she quickly gulped down the water from the bottle in her hand and reached for the hanging frying pan on the rack above the kitchen island. With just a few quick motions, she dropped the pan on the burner. "How about some eggs?" She flipped on the burner and everything went from bright orange to gray as the explosion ripped through the house and then collapsed through the foundation.

chapter **41**

DOWN, DOWN, DOWN they all fell: all the pieces of the Lawsons and the pieces of their home fell into the sinkhole that had been expanding beneath their house. What would have naturally happened in a month's time, had been accelerated by the explosion. The house was engulphed in flame, the impact caused the small amount of ground cover straining to hold up the house to finally give way. Perhaps if their debt and their moral bankruptcies could have turned into steel beams or simply piles of bullion, their house could have been supported by that massive pile of financial waste. If all the pennies and dimes of their debt were deposited below that house, perhaps it would have stayed, the foundation might not have cracked.

But, unfortunately, all of that money was sitting, weighing on the structure. That money was there in the form of expensive furniture and cars, items, junk, all weighing on the frame of the home. Not even the entirety of the 12 trillion dollars in US consumer debt converted into nickels and then soldered together to create beams to support the structure would have saved that house. The weight was just too heavy, the hole too wide, the damage too far gone.

As for Jack and his wife, they were so sad to hear about the Lawsons and the sinkhole. Since the new owners had technically taken ownership of their former house that week, they were under no obligation to the house or the neighborhood and could continue their drive, unencumbered by things, debt, or worry.

The video posted by the Ryechik's on the day of their party had already received several hundred views by the time the Lawson's house exploded. Once the news began to cover the multiple theories of the case, they latched onto the suspect timing of the Ryechiks moving away. Science had, in fact, confirmed that the sinkhole that had developed as a result of the Hydroline mineral drilling had caused the foundation of the house to crumble. When the gas lines broke, the house began to fill with noxious fumes. As the structure fell, the materials began to spark, causing the first and then the second explosions.

Another conspiracy theory that made its rounds on the internet was that Mr. Lawson had intended to have the house collapse with Cynthia inside it to pay off his debt. This was too juicy to be ignored, although no one would ever be able to confirm that this was true. The other theory that the neighbors, the Ryechiks, had something to do with it garnered even more attention. Everyone loves a good scandal, no one really wants the banal truth anymore.

Their creditors lost quite a bit when the Lawsons perished, taking with them years and years of fee income and future spending.

Henrietta refused to believe the incident report when it was finally released. Henri was convinced that Cynthia must have done something drastic to cause this. She had been so unstable and irrational. When the rumors surfaced that Lawson look-a-likes were spotted, she nearly drove herself to the edge of madness trying to find her cousin alive somewhere.

What had become so commonplace was the expectation of something unbelievable. The headline-grabbing extra-ordinary was just another day of updates on the social feed. What really killed the Lawsons is the same thing that kills us all, kills our souls: the focus on the status and the money and not on the people around us.

But, why be shocked by that? Why be mystified at what happened to the Lawsons? Was their demise not clearly explained to you, was the ticking clock not apparent? In the pages that you've read through, you've been able to see what about the Lawsons made them likable and what made they repugnant. So, this ending has nothing to do with them, they are gone. It has to do with you. Were you devouring each word, excited about their forthcoming demise? Or, were you hopeful? Against all odds, did you root for their redemption? The house on Hurley Pond and the dreams sold along with it are common dreams. In light of what happened to the Lawsons, what are your uncommon dreams?

"That's what we're setting out to do, we're going to see so much of the world that we become sick of traveling, we are going to help those in need until our efforts are futile, we're going to go out and see, and explore, and try to get those most out of this one life." —FIRE Day Video Post, Checkin' Out with the Ryechiks, uploaded July 12 5:00 PM EST. 1,356,000 views.

THE END

ABOUT THE AUTHOR

M.K. Williams is the author of multiple books. You can follow her for more in-depth information on these books at 1mkwilliams.com. To receive updates on upcoming books, please take a moment to subscribe.

If you enjoyed this story, please consider leaving a review for Enemies of Peace. Each review helps other readers discover this book. Thank you for your support.